AWAKENED

David Berardelli

AWAKENED

GRAVESTONE PRESS

ISBN: 978 1 78695 782 5

Gravestone Press
is an imprint of
Fiction4All
www.fiction4all.com

This Edition
Published 2022

Cover Art: Linda York

DEDICATION

This book is dedicated to treasured memories of
Andi, Poncho, Tapper, Wiffle, Kylie, Misty,
Kirby,
and Misty Girl

All wonderful dogs, all wonderful memories

PART 1 - THE FIRST DAY

Chapter 1

The doctors told him out in the hall outside her room that there was no change. After nearly three months, his wife remained in a coma.

He had almost gone into the room to see her, just as he had done every single day for the last three months. This time, however, he decided not to. Seeing her lying there so still and lifeless, hooked up to tubes, destroyed him, firing up every single fiber of his being while turning his blood ice-cold.

He realized this time that he could no longer put himself through this agony. Looking at her pale, cold features numbed him, shedding him of all hope and filling his soul with an overpowering darkness he had never encountered before. This time, he'd stopped in his tracks just a step or two short of the doorway and stood there, stock-still, staring at the dirty tile at his feet while listening once again to their bleak news.

When the throbbing in his head finally eased up, he took a few deep, labored breaths and closed his eyes. After what seemed an eternity, the chaos within him eventually grew slightly more distant and diminished in intensity. When he thought he was ready to return to cold reality, he turned around. His legs were stiff and heavy as he shuffled back down the corridor, which led to the elevators that would take him down to the ground floor…and then

7

the exit…and the lobby…and eventually the outside world, where he'd be forced to face another day alone in the apartment, surrounded by her things, her scent, her touch…

But without her.

They asked him just the other day if he wanted to switch off the machines. If he wanted to stop her pain, her agony. If he was ready to begin his future without her at his side. They had been closely examining the monitors for several weeks and were all in agreement that her condition would most likely never improve.

Stop her pain. Turn her off. Call it a day. Let her go. Make the decision that would forever rip his heart right out of his chest.

Turn her off. As if she was nothing more than a kitchen appliance that no longer functioned properly.

Hell no, he thought, the memories cascading wildly in his brain. Her face. Her body. Her smile. Her touch. Her soft voice. The way she kissed him, made love to him, talked to him, treated him. Teased him. How she knew what he was thinking, what he would say even before he had said it aloud. How she brushed her hair, applied her makeup. How her face lit up with a smile whenever she caught him watching her dress in front of the full-length mirror. How she always had trouble flipping open the tab on the mustard container without splashing herself. The times he had made a mess on the kitchen counter because he hadn't noticed that she'd forgotten to tighten the cap on the olive oil bottle the last time she used it.

The day they first met at the company picnic at Lake Nona that took place more than eight years ago would be forever etched in his memory.

"I'm Morgan," she announced, walking right up to him and stopping just two feet away, smiling that bright dimpled smile he'd fallen in love with so quickly. "Morgan Lee. I'm their artwork and graphics girl."

Her proud, confident manner startled and amazed him. She had just appeared, looking beautiful and animated in her maroon shorts and gold tank top, her long, toned legs tanned to a golden brown from the Central Florida sun. He'd been so surprised by her glow that every single thought in his head jumped ship, leaving him helplessly silent with her standing so close, her bright smile penetrating his spirit and sending a sensation of caressing warmth billowing through him.

"You're Owen, right?" Her voice had somehow penetrated the thick silence which had instantly turned him into a block of insecurity. "Owen Roth?"

When reality finally returned, sending with it a message that he should at least try to react in some sensible way, he decided that he should give this beauty some clear sign that he wasn't dead or nearly as unconscious as he appeared. He hoped his brain was still working and that he should at least try and let her know that he wasn't as lifeless as he seemed. Struggling to regain some of the dignity he was reasonably sure he still possessed, he took a breath and cleared his throat as subtly as possible. "That's what my driver's license says," he said awkwardly, and felt his pulse pumping harder than he ever imagined possible.

She laughed at his response—which told him that he'd either totally humiliated himself or said something clever. Since she hadn't immediately spun around and run away laughing hysterically, he assumed he hadn't convinced her that he was an idiot.

"I've seen you in the reception area several times," she said, still smiling. "You usually come in and talk with Stephanie, our buyer."

The image immediately blipped in his head, and before he realized it, coherent thought—as well as speech—had finally come to the rescue. "The tall, skinny blonde with the heavy makeup, pricey wardrobe, and horrible perfume?"

She laughed again, this time harder. "That's Stephanie, all right."

"Sorry if I—"

"It's all right." Then she turned, possibly to see if Stephanie was within earshot. When she turned back to him, she lowered her voice. "You've obviously never flirted with her."

She'd said it as if it was an accusation. He didn't know how—or if—he should reply.

"It's true, isn't it?"

He sighed and hoped he wouldn't sound smug. "I'm afraid so."

She looked confused. "Everyone flirts with Stephanie. I mean everyone. Why haven't you?"

The woman was arrogant and self-absorbed, and he clearly remembered the number of times she mentioned her membership with the local spa after complimenting him on how good he looked in a suit. He didn't like women who were so obvious or outspoken.

Morgan lowered her voice once again. "You can tell me, you know." She frowned, wrinkling her nose. "I don't really like her. Most of us don't. She's so…snooty. She also has a facelift or tummy tuck every time she goes on vacation."

He didn't know if he should comment, so he just nodded.

"Why haven't you joined the Stephanie fanbase? She likes you, you know. She has a type. It's usually a fit-looking, well-dressed, nice-looking guy with good hair and—well, someone just like you."

He puffed up at her apparent compliment and tried hard not to grin like an idiot. This told him that she probably liked him, but he knew better than act stupid—which could easily change her mind. He just shrugged. "I just don't like her."

"Why not?"

"She's…well, like I said, her perfume's really horrible."

Morgan smiled.

"I mean it. She was standing awfully close to me the other day. That stuff she was wearing made me want to look for the nearest hazmat suit. I grew nauseous and would have thrown up on her business suit if I hadn't been so afraid of grossing out everyone standing around."

She laughed and pushed back a knot of shiny chestnut hair that had slipped in front of her cheekbone. "Is that the *main* reason? The perfume thing?"

He just shrugged.

"You're saying yes?"

"I didn't say anything. I just shrugged."

She blinked. "And just what does that shrug mean, Mr. Owen Roth?"

Her saying his name did something to him, and he realized in that single moment that this woman was special. The rare type of girl he didn't want to let slip through his fingers. And when he said, "Could be that I knew the moment I first saw her that I wasn't gonna waste my time," he knew by the dimples marking her cheeks that this woman was one of those once-in-a-lifetime babes a guy with the usual amount of normal brain activity just didn't pass up.

That wondrous event had happened more than eight years ago, when he was twenty-seven and she twenty-five. The company picnic had brought two Central Florida companies together to complete a long-awaited merger. His firm, Collins & Sons, specialized in the beautification of public gardens, while ImageFlorida, where Morgan worked, dealt with local advertising. Both firms were small, each boasting just twenty or so employees. With spouses and children, turnout for the picnic that day barely amounted to eighty in attendance.

But the only thing he really cared about that day was Morgan Lee and how fantastic she looked in her shorts, tank top, and open-toed sandals, her thick chestnut hair that glistened in the Florida

12

sunlight, and how great her long, shapely tanned legs filled the bright picture screen in his head.

And her dazzling smile. But above all, her laugh, which was music to his ears, warming him all over.

He didn't remember much at all about the picnic. There were the usual rah-rah speeches, as there were with any other company picnic. There was also plenty of food, and the beer had been brought over in kegs, along with half a dozen cases of cold drinks, and three large coolers stacked with blocks of ice. He didn't even remember what he ate, or even if he had eaten at all. All that filled his mind that day was the tall, slender, chestnut-haired beauty who had shared that day with him. That very special babe who left the picnic in her small copper Honda Accord and followed him to his Winter Park apartment, where she captured his heart as well as his spirit in a very short period of time.

Now, as he left the hospital to begin the long, agonizing walk back to his car, he could think only of the last few months, which now seemed like a lifetime, beginning with the call by the OPD to inform him that Morgan had been involved in a serious highway accident and that she'd been rushed to Orlando Regional Hospital, where she was placed in ICU due to brain trauma.

On his way back to their apartment, he stopped at the intersection of Semoran and Colonial, where the accident had happened. He pulled into the side turnoff of the Mall, parked, then switched off the ignition. Then, for the next twenty minutes, he stared numbly at the heavy traffic and once again visualized the scene that had taken the love of his life away from him and turned her into the cold, lifeless form now hooked up to machines in a depressingly white, sanitized room.

"T-boned," the cop on the scene had told him the moment he'd reached the hospital directly from the office, where he'd been in conference with his bosses, watching six middle-aged execs in expensive suits droning on loudly about some mindless company policy that made no sense whatsoever. "According to an eyewitness, she'd just proceeded through green to head north on Semoran when the silver Lexus moving west ran the light and slammed into her. Luckily, the idiot was only going twenty when he hit her. Otherwise?" The cop shrugged and looked disgusted.

Otherwise…

That one word left quite a bit to the imagination. Otherwise, in this sense, meant a great many things, none of them promising or even tolerable. Otherwise meant, in one sense, that if the idiot had been moving slightly faster, Morgan would have surely died. Or have been paralyzed. Or slammed even more brutally into the driver's window, where she would have most certainly suffered massive facial and head injuries.

Since the idiot slamming into her hadn't been going very fast, the fact that Morgan was now lying in a hospital bed, hooked up to a battery of tubes keeping her organs functioning, seemed much, much better.

Didn't it?

14

Wasn't that what life was all about? Survival? Beating the Grim Reaper? Making it through another day? Keeping the organs from winding down and then shutting off completely?

He sat there in his usual cold, empty numbness, staring unseeingly at the constantly moving traffic while thinking of what had happened, and of the drunken idiot who had put her where she'd been the last three months. Then, after opening the console between the seats, he picked up the Smith & Wesson .45 revolver he had bought five years ago at the pawnshop on South Orange Blossom Trail. His pulse hastening, he checked the cylinder before snapping it shut and placing it back into its niche.

His nerves sizzled as he pulled back onto the highway, heading west, for Parkway Towers Condominiums, the fancy apartment building on West Colonial, where the bastard who had destroyed the love of his life lived in luxury. And as he got back into traffic, he told himself that this dirtbag would be dead before the night ended.

Chapter 2

Owen parked the Challenger on Broadway Avenue, across the street from the Parkway Towers, and sat staring at the rows of vehicles parked in the lot in front of the eighteen-story building.

The high-rise appeared as it always had—slightly weathered, its sandblasted face smudged with dust and grime from years of traffic and the elements. Palms and trimmed hedges embellished the block. Two young, slender figures walked down the street, smoking cigarettes. A middle-aged woman in a jogging suit wandered down Colonial, her Golden Retriever leading the way on a leash. Traffic went by.

It was just a few minutes before eleven when a figure appeared from the building. The streetlamp lighting up the entrance showed that the figure was Hargrove. The man immediately walked down the paved aisle, where his vehicle, a new Lexus to replace the one he had damaged by smashing into Morgan's Honda, was parked. Dressed impeccably as usual, he adjusted the knot of his tie as he marched down the paved drive, whistling.

One of the conditions of Hargrove's release was that he stayed away from bars and stopped drinking completely for a period of not less than six months. Though the accident with Morgan had taken place three months ago, Hargrove, as Owen had personally observed, had spent considerable time in bars, raising elbows with friends and wealthy investors during the last three or four weeks.

Owen's heart began thrashing wildly. His blood quickly heated up as he opened the console. With a shaky hand, he groped for the .45.

As he held it in his hand, he noticed how much heavier it seemed. How much colder the metal felt. Although he had owned the gun for the last several years, it felt so foreign to him right now that he was tempted to switch on the interior light to see if something strange had happened. If some unseen force, for some unknown reason, had switched it with something bigger, something much heavier, more deadly.

It was his imagination stepping in. The good part of his soul was rebelling against the evil. The darkness that automatically took over the moment he first saw Morgan lying comatose in her hospital bed and decided that the bastard responsible would die.

He *had* to die, and he would die tonight.

Then what? that cursed inner voice asked, as he clutched the revolver much more tightly and felt the skin of his palm melting into the wooden grip.

It doesn't matter, he told the voice.

You can just walk away from this, you know...

I don't want to.

Really?

Maybe now that I know that she's never coming home, that things will never be the way they once were... Maybe I won't want to go home and spend the rest of my life all alone...

Are you sure?

17

Yes.

He switched off the voice before giving it more of a chance to change his mind. While watching the cursed figure venturing down the aisle, he pushed open the door of the Challenger.

The warm September night breeze gently caressed his sensitive flesh, and he shivered. Taking a deep breath, he quickly found his total purpose centered on the idiot who had slammed into Morgan.

This was the despicable moron that, with the help of the team of law experts who specialized in vehicular homicide and involuntary manslaughter cases, had been given a suspended sentence.

But none of that mattered. The only thing that did matter was that the bastard was going to die tonight.

The .45 gripped tightly in his hand, Owen silently got out of the Challenger. After easing the door shut, he marched across the street, his focus on the dark figure getting out his keys, just a hundred feet away.

His blood began to boil all over again. He took another deep breath and forced himself to concentrate on the job at hand.

As he moved, the warm, irresistible memories

("I've seen you in the reception area several times")

swam around vigorously

("And just what does that shrug mean, Mr. Owen Roth?")

in his head.

His pulse hammered violently; he began shaking. *Steady. Just a few more seconds. Then it will be all over. Morgan will remain comatose, but at least the idiot who put her in that hospital bed won't be out there, threatening other people's lives.*

At least that was *something*…

Sighing deeply, he raised his arm. Then, steadying the gun with his other hand, he aimed the four-inch barrel.

Hargrove was now standing beside the driver's door, fiddling with his keys. The left side of his head was in clear view, less than a hundred feet away.

A hundred feet was nothing. A hundred feet was a bull's eye he could manage at any shooting range all day long, day or night. A hundred feet was a comfortable distance for him. The kick of the .45 was substantial, but he was used to it. He'd been proficient with large caliber guns for years.

This one's for you, Morgan, he thought as his eyes welled with hot tears. *This is your one and only chance at vengeance. You can't do it yourself, so I'm gonna do it for you.*

Then, as he had learned years ago, when his father, a Vietnam vet, taught him how to shoot, he slowly expelled all the air from his lungs and began applying slightly more pressure to the trigger.

Just then, a soft, high-pitched whimper close to his left side startled him. He dropped his arms and spun sharply toward the source of the sound.

A dog was sitting on its haunches about three feet away, watching him intently.

19

The back of his neck grew hot, and he stiffened. Then, bringing the gun to his right side and carefully depressing the hammer, he waited for his pulse to return to normal.

The dog was large—about forty or fifty pounds. In the haze of the streetlight at the corner its coat looked brown and white, but he knew this meant that it could be gold, or even red. The animal looked like some sort of Aussie mix. He couldn't see a collar or tag and assumed it must be a stray. But since it wasn't skinny or weak looking, he didn't think it had been on its own very long.

However, the dog's size, shape or pedigree were not the issue here. It had approached him silently and purposefully. And for some strange reason he could not comprehend, it seemed to sense what he was about to do.

When reality nudged him back to the present, he realized that this stray had just upset his plan. He always loved dogs but hadn't owned one in many years. Morgan had been a dog-lover all her life and had lost her beloved yellow Lab Hannah just months before he met her. The loss had devastated her so much that she hadn't wanted to own a dog ever since.

He needed to make the dog go away. He couldn't possibly kill Hargrove while this animal was sitting right here, staring at him. It had already distracted him, and for this, a distraction would be the kiss of death. But all was not lost. It appeared to be a stray and would probably scare away easily.

"Are you lost?"

The dog continued staring.

"Where are your people?" Owen glanced up and down the street. He saw no one. "Your owners? Your mom? Your dad? A little kid you just ran away from because he wasn't paying attention and you weren't that fond of him anyway?"

The dog continued staring at him.

"I know it's late and all, but even so, you seem to be all alone." He realized he was talking to a dog and that he could not possibly get much of an acknowledgement, but he didn't know what else to do. "Can you possibly give me any sort of hint as to where—which direction—you came from?"

No reaction.

He glanced across the street. Hargrove had already gotten in the Lexus.

Owen sighed tiredly but was confident he could still manage a shot if Hargrove drove up the ramp leading to Colonial. It would be a straight shot to the windshield, but the revolver was loaded with full metal jackets, which would easily penetrate safety glass.

"You really need to go back home, wherever that is. I'm about to do something very bad, and you can't be here for this. Unless you're a hunting dog, the sound of this gun will probably scare the hell out of you, not to mention hurt your ears. You know what they say about a dog's hearing, right?"

The dog continued staring. Its eyes didn't shift from him.

"I don't mean to be rude, but please go away. I mean it. If I do what I came here to do, this area will be a madhouse in just a few minutes. Get it? People

21

and traffic all over the damned place. You might get hurt or run over if you stick around."

Still no reaction.

"Don't you have anywhere else you should be?" Owen shrugged. "Your people's home? Your doghouse in the backyard?"

The steady hum of a vehicle increased in volume as it drifted up the ramp, in his direction. At that same moment, two cars headed down Broadway, making their way for Colonial.

His pulse skipped a beat. He needed to be invisible.

"No offense, but I've got to go. Nice chatting with you. And *please* don't wander onto the road and get run over. It would tear me apart to see you lying there, turned into roadkill."

Again, no reaction.

Forcing his attention away from the dog, Owen hurried down the street, toward his car. He stopped halfway down the block, out of range of the streetlights and near an untrimmed bush. In seconds, the Lexus reached the end of the drive. Then, without pause, it turned left and shot in front of fast-moving traffic on Colonial.

He watched the silver blur and felt his grip tightening around the grip of the .45. It took a conscious effort to pull his finger away from the trigger. *Another day, you bastard*, he sent after the fleeing car. *Next time, you won't luck out because I won't let anything distract me again.*

A slight whimper broke the silence directly behind him.

He turned.

The dog was sitting as it had before, staring up at him.

Chapter 3

The dog followed him back to the Challenger.

Once again, he was faced with a serious dilemma. He knew he couldn't possibly get in the car and leave the animal. This was a busy area. The heavy traffic—as well as the arrogance and incompetence of most drivers—worried him. He couldn't live with himself if he thought even for a moment that this dog might not survive the night.

"You didn't exactly go home as I suggested, did you?" he asked the dog.

The animal cocked its head as it watched him.

"You know how I know? You're sitting right here, just a couple of feet away from me. To me, that's clear proof that you're nowhere else."

No reaction.

"Listen. I've got to leave now. I can't spend the night talking to you. For one thing, you're not talking back. You're not telling me anything I really need to know. In other words, I don't know what I'm supposed to do about you."

The dog licked its lips and glanced at a passing car, then turned back to him.

He wondered if he should take the dog to the nearest shelter.

"You wouldn't like what I'm thinking right now."

Silence.

"I'm thinking of taking you to a shelter."

No reaction.

"I know of one not far from here. It's not a kill shelter, so they'll take care of you until someone comes in and takes a shine to you."

Silence.

"It won't take long at all. You're a sweet, good-looking animal. You've got the kind of eyes that would make most people melt. I've already melted, and believe me, I'm not exactly the type who melts—especially not lately. You're what I'd call beautiful. I'd take you home, but I wouldn't be what you'd call very good company. Besides, I have some really awful things I need to do..." He sighed and considered his options. This was not the time for him to be distracted. He had reached the end of his rope and needed immediate release. Taking in a dog at this point in his life would not be sensible. "Listen, I'm really not in the position to take in a dog right now. My life is a total mess, I'm about to do something to end things very shortly, and it wouldn't be very bright or humane to take you in and then leave you all alone in the apartment."

Silence.

He rubbed his eyes and struggled to stay focused. This dog had no idea what he was going through. There was no reason for him to spend time trying to reason with an animal that had no clue how his life had collapsed. "My wife's in the hospital, and it doesn't look good. I couldn't be a very good dad for you. I mean it. Under different circumstances? Maybe. But not now. It's not your fault, it's just that—"

Home...

A bright image of his apartment flashed in his head, and he immediately forgot what he was talking about. He fought off the confusion. What the hell was happening? Why did he suddenly see a flash of his place in his mind? "Home?" he muttered.

The dog's soft "*woof*" made him cringe.

He stared at the animal in tense silence, wondering what had just happened. Was this his imagination? Or had this canine somehow transmitted a clear image of his apartment into his head?

This was silly. And totally unrealistic.

How could this stray project a strange image into his brain?

His emotions were in overload again. It was because of the accident. The trauma. The damned nightmare taking root. This dog could not possibly be communicating telepathically with him. It couldn't know anything about his apartment or where he lived, so how could it be responsible for the flash?

Get real!

But just to make sure, he stared at the dog and said, "Home?"

Once again, the dog woofed softly. Its short nub of a tail swished furiously on the pavement.

"*Your* home?"

No reaction.

"You wanna come home with me?"

Another "woof," this time much more emphatic.

He realized right then that he was not taking this dog to the shelter.

***

The dog sat in the passenger seat, gazing at the windshield as Owen drove the Challenger.

He kept glancing at the dog. It seemed alert and happy, but also very vulnerable and a little anxious. He felt sorry for it and wanted to tell it everything would turn out all right.

But he couldn't. Not with a clear conscience. All right just wasn't the way things were. Life had the nasty habit of turning brutally hard at the most inopportune moment. Most of the time, things just didn't turn out the way you wanted them to. Horrible stuff happened. Just a few months ago, he and Morgan were living happy, carefree lives. Their offices were only a block from one another on Maguire Boulevard. Their hours were basically the same. They frequently shared lunch at Fashion Square, or one of the steakhouses or seafood places on Colonial Drive. They went to work together and drove home together. Most of the time, they had their weekends free and could enjoy one another's company at the complex pool, on the tennis court, shopping for groceries, driving to one of the many antique shops in the area, or simply relaxing in the apartment and watching their favorite movies on DVD or on Netflix.

But after eight years of marital bliss, life unexpectedly turned around and then flipped upside-down. Morgan lay comatose in a hospital bed and he, after taking a voluntary leave from Collins & Sons, spent his days sitting on the living

27

room couch, drinking bourbon while plotting to murder the monster responsible for destroying his life.

How in hell could he tell anyone—even a stray dog that had suddenly entered his life—that everything would be okay, fantastic, and blissful again?

"I'm taking you to OPD," he said softly, staring at the road straight ahead.

He felt horrible the moment the words left his throat. It was no better than telling a lost little boy that he was going to be dropped off at the bus stop and left there. But he didn't want to leave the dog and didn't want it to be hit by traffic or taken by some moron to be sold later on and used as bait for dog fighting. And he had no idea what else he could do. "It's the Police Station. They're nice there. A great bunch of guys. They'll try and find you a place to stay."

Incredibly, the animal turned to look at him. Even in the darkness of the cab he could tell that it disapproved of what he just said.

"I can't just *leave* you, ya know." He had to justify this—to himself as well as to the dog. "That would be cruel. Anyway, this is not by any means personal. I happen to love dogs. I couldn't just drop you off, hightail it, and forget all about you." He sighed. "If you only knew what I've been going through—"

As if it understood him, the dog whined softly.

"I just don't know what else to do, dammit..."

Another soft whine.

28

"Is there some reason why I shouldn't take you to the police station?"

No reaction.

"All right, then. Let's try this another way. Where *would* you like me to take you?"

Silence.

"If you don't want the police to help you…"

No response.

You're being ridiculous. You're trying to reason with a dog, for God's sake. Sure, dogs are bright… But listen to you. You're talking to it as if it's an actual person.

Not knowing how else he could handle this, he said, "Where *would* you like to go?"

No response.

"How about if I take you home? Where I live?"

A soft "woof." Then, as if on cue, the dog slumped in the seat. Its face was tilted toward him as it closed its eyes and relaxed.

29

Chapter 4

It was nearly midnight when Owen pulled into his parking space facing the two-story Winter Park condo he and Morgan had been sharing since they were married.

The dog hadn't moved. He flicked off the ignition and watched it, wondering once again what he should do. This situation was very strange. He felt sorry for the animal but realized this was not the right time for him to be distracted from what he intended to do with Hargrove. He knew cops treated dogs well but still didn't want to go that route. Despite his confusion and the horror he'd endured during the last three months, he couldn't shake the strong feeling that dropping off this dog would be a very bad thing to do.

What was this "strong feeling?"

Was this intuition? Was it dread? Was he afraid that if he did take the dog somewhere, he'd worry that he'd done the wrong thing and would soon be torn up with guilt?

He knew the type of person he was. He knew damned well that the moment he dropped this dog off, he wouldn't be able to concentrate on anything else.

What other option was there? It was getting late, and the possibilities had greatly diminished. Dropping off this dog seemed out of the question. He knew that he was incapable of doing such a thing.

Where did this leave him?

30

The answer was both simple and disturbing. He had to take the dog inside. Hopefully, it was housebroken. If so, he could make a bed for it and feed it in the morning. If not, he would work on some other strategy. His apartment boasted a fenced-in backyard, but it was small. He could take the dog for a walk to the picnic area at the other end of the complex property just beyond the tennis court. Morgan still kept the leash and collar she'd bought for Hannah. Since this dog was slightly smaller, the collar would fit. He just hoped the animal wouldn't give him any trouble when he tried putting it on.

He wondered how Morgan would feel about all this. Morgan was not only beautiful, bright, and perceptive, she was also tolerant, but had little patience for nasty or negative people. However, she had never been able to overcome her grief for Hannah, and if a miracle happened and she was able to return home, she might not accept a strange dog. But he knew she'd definitely want him to help this animal and would never forgive him if she learned that he'd come across a stray and hadn't gone to every length possible to find out where it had come from.

His mind made up, he reached over.

Just before he could touch the dog's shoulder, it stirred, sat up, and stared at him.

"I'm the guy you shanghaied on Broadway Avenue. Not really shanghaied, exactly…but you know what I mean."

No response.

"We're home."

31

The dog seemed to smile. A soft, gentle "woof" left its throat.

"I take it you're okay with that, then?"

No reaction.

"You'll be all right. It's a two-bedroom, and you can sleep anywhere."

Silence.

Now was the time for the big question.

"Are you, by any chance, housebroken?"

The dog tilted its head.

"What I mean is, do you have to pee? Or make a few sizeable deposits around the property?"

No response.

"All right, then. I guess there's one sure way to find out." He pulled the .45 out of the console, turned, and pushed open the door. The dog jumped down and stood there, sniffing and checking out the new surroundings. It trotted over to one of the bushes beneath his living room window, where it squatted, then straightened moments later.

Owen smiled. "You must be a lady dog."

"Woof..."

"I didn't know if you were housebroken."

A soft whine.

"Sorry I doubted you. I suspected you had some dignity, but I couldn't be quite sure."

She tilted her head.

"What I meant was, I'm just...well, I guess I'm just babbling."

"Woof..."

He went up the three stone steps and unlocked the front door. The moment he pushed it open, the dog trotted inside.

***

In the foyer lighting, the dog's coat exhibited a golden-brown color, with patches of gold covering her sides and butt.

Her four-inch nub of tail was light brown. Her ears were tipped. Her left ear was a speckled white, the right, a golden-brown. Her face was peppered with flecks of gold amongst the white, with larger brown freckles on her skull as well as her throat. Her thick coat appeared incredibly soft. Her eyes were a soft light brown. A sincere gentleness and warmth in her expression made him feel less anxious and much more relaxed.

"No," he said, smiling at her, "I don't think Morgan would have approved of me dropping you off anywhere."

The dog's head tilted again.

"Frankly, Owen wouldn't have, either."

She opened her mouth and seemed to smile.

He walked past her and went down the lit hall leading to the kitchen. He turned on the overhead light and was placing the .45 in the top drawer of the cabinet when she followed him in.

"Hungry?" He closed the drawer and watched as she sat down in front of him and let her tongue slide out of her mouth.

"I imagine you must be thirsty." He found one of Morgan's porcelain bowls in the cupboard, rinsed it out at the sink, poured fresh water into it and set it carefully on the floor inside the doorway, beneath the small desk Morgan used to balance their bank account.

As if on cue, the dog went right over and began drinking.

"You *were* thirsty, weren'tcha?"

The dog stopped drinking, turned, and sat staring up at him. She seemed to be smiling again.

"Now you look hungry."

No reaction.

"I don't have any dog food." He shrugged. "This happens when people don't have an actual dog living with them." He went to the fridge, opened a drawer, and took out a package of shredded black forest ham he used for sandwiches and omelets. He opened the package, pulled out about a cup, and dropped it in a small bowl. Then he took it over and placed it next to the water dish. "Hope you like ham." He smiled. "It's seven and a half bucks a pound, by the way. Not that you'd care, but…" He shrugged.

The dog trotted over, sniffed the bowl, then attacked the ham, devouring it in seconds.

"Let me guess. You're not a gourmet."

The dog burped, then had another slug of water.

"Don't feel bad. I'm not, either." He opened the cabinet door and pulled out a bottle half-filled with bourbon. He poured an inch into a glass and set down the bottle. He drained the glass and was pleased that the stuff had more of a kick to it than usual. It was only then that he realized how exhausted he was. "If you don't mind, I think I'll call it a day."

The dog tilted her head and watched him intently.

"I didn't think you would." He put the bottle back and went down the hall. The dog followed, stopping a few feet away from him as he reached the sofa. "Are you, by any chance, a couch dog?"

No reaction.

"You look relatively clean, so if you want to sleep on the couch, have at it."

The dog yawned.

Owen nodded. "Well, if you don't mind, I'm already halfway to la-la land." He made his way for the stairs. He switched off the living room light and the room immediately faded into a soft gray darkness. The night light in the hall and kitchen counter backsplash lighting provided an orange haze that lit up portions of the tiled floor.

"Good night, pretty lady."

For a moment he wondered if she had given him a soft whine in reply. Then he realized he was just tired. He heard a lot of weird things when he was tired and had learned long ago not to let it bother him too much. As Morgan always told him, "Don't sweat the little things."

With a deep sigh, he staggered up the carpeted steps.

Chapter 5

Brent Hargrove pulled the Lexus into his spot in the parking lot of the Parkway Towers, doused the lights and flicked off the ignition.

His blood pounding, he spent the next couple of minutes salivating over the luscious babe sitting in the leather seat beside him, her delicious jugs making him so uncomfortable, he didn't think he'd be able to make it to the eighteenth floor in time. He was slightly drunk, but not so far gone that his senses couldn't respond to the sweet-smelling beauty staring back at him so dangerously close, her green eyes focused on his mouth, her parted lips suggesting things he could only imagine in his wildest, most sex-induced dreams...

Lana was her name. Lana Drake, who danced part-time at one of the better clubs in Winter Park when she wasn't handling calls at CF Investments, Inc., where Brent had been working the last ten years as an investment counselor. At five-nine, she passed six feet in her spiked heels, those perfectly sculpted legs mesmerizing him each time his gaze wandered in their direction. And with those gorgeous jugs, she knew damned well that she could have any guy she ever wanted. But tonight, she wanted him, and he was hellbent on making her desires—as well as his own—come true.

"You're staring," she said softly, gently nudging some thick black ringlets away from her swelled cheekbone. "It's, well, kind of embarrassing."

As much as he wanted to, he could not take his eyes off those jugs. Here he was, thirty-six years old, a college grad working for one of the most prestigious brokerages in Central Florida, with an extremely impressive personal portfolio. But with this babe, he felt as if he'd gone back in time, when he was fifteen, watching his first porno DVD, the urgent hard-on mashing against his jeans making the slightest movement excruciating. Lana was one of those babes who was used to getting along on her looks. Hell, all the guys at CF Investments lusted after her. And like everyone else, he also knew she spent her time only with guys who could do her some good. But he didn't care. The thing he cared about was that she had gone out with him and was now sitting here in his car. He could tell by her body language—and by her attitude—that she was eager to accompany him up to his penthouse suite. And they both knew what that meant.

"Can't help it," he told her. "You're quite an eyeful." He could clearly imagine how those jugs would look naked. He couldn't wait much longer to get her out of those clothes so he could see for himself. But he'd been around the block a few times and knew that if a guy wanted to get into a high-quality babe's pants, he needed to let her man the helm—at least for the time being. When babes thought they were in control, they went crazy and pushed the envelope whichever way they pleased.

"You know what the girls at the office say about you, don'tcha?"

Although he knew full well what she meant, he wanted to hear it coming from those luscious lips anyway. "What do they say?"

"You're trouble."

He laughed. "I should hope so. I've spent most of my adult life trying to get everything just right."

She lowered her eyes to his lap, and he felt his body temperature leap a few more degrees. "I'm wondering if being here with you is gonna turn out to be a good career move."

"That depends on if you're a good girl or a very bad one."

"What's the difference?"

"You don't know?"

She smiled. "I'd like to hear your version."

"If you're a good girl, you'll let me start the ball rolling so I can do whatever the hell I want."

"And if I'm bad?"

"Well, you could always take things into your own hands. If you know what I mean…"

She shook her head. "You really *are* trouble, ya know…"

He moved toward her, and they kissed, long and passionately. He knew right then that he wouldn't be able to last much longer. He needed to take her up to his suite and get his damned clothes off before he humiliated himself. "I think it's time for bed," he whispered in her face.

She licked her lips. "I'm not at all sleepy…"

"I said *bed*—not *sleep*. There's a difference, right? A *big* one…"

"I guess that all depends on who I'm with."

"Baby, you're not gonna get much sleep tonight. Bank on it."

"I had no idea you were psychic."

"Just a damned good guesser."

"That's probably why you're so great at knowing the Market."

"I've done tons and tons of field research, you could say."

"Is *that* what they're calling it now?"

"It's one way of putting it."

"I guess it's time for me to check out the field, then."

"Well *past* time." He opened his door and got out. Then, forcing himself to stay calm, he circled the Lexus. It wasn't long at all before he experienced the same eerie feeling as a few hours earlier. A very strong feeling that someone was watching him.

He first felt it when he'd made it halfway down the aisle of the lot and seen the guy standing on the sidewalk directly across the street. The strange thing was that he thought he'd seen only *one* figure at first. But just a moment later, he decided that the streetlight—as well as the passing traffic—were doing a number on him, creating shadows.

He was watching a man and what looked like a dog. Neither was staring at him. And although this alone should have made him feel less tense, he experienced the same unsettling sensation once he'd gotten into the car, brought it up the exit ramp, then pulled out onto Colonial.

Strange. A man and a dog standing on the sidewalk. In this neighborhood, such a sight happened frequently, even at this time of night.

Why was this bothering him so much?

It made him think briefly of what had happened three months earlier, when he slammed into that Honda.

Guilt, maybe? Or was he just a little stressed?

At the moment, he could think only of his libido. And the delicious babe getting out of the Lexus.

Didn't matter. Once they'd gotten into bed and did the deed, he'd start feeling like his old self again. After all, it had been more than a week since he'd last been laid. A guy with his looks, wallet, and lifestyle didn't take too kindly to a ten-day dry spell.

"How new is your car?" she asked suddenly.

"Why do you ask?"

"It's got that new car smell that lingers for a while."

"I got it three months ago."

"After your accident?"

"Yeah…" It was time to take her up to his pad, strip her, get her down on the bed and do the deed. He wasn't in the mood for this kind of talk. He needed sex—not another reminder of what had happened. Once she had two or three more drinks in her, she'd have different things on her mind, such as getting out of his bedroom in one piece. The thought of it made his pulse hammer.

"Let's go inside and I'll show you my etchings."

40

She blinked. "You really *have* those?"

He shrugged. "I thought I'd be subtle for a change."

Giggling, she moved closer and he took her hand.

41

PART 2 - THE SECOND DAY

Chapter 6

Brent Hargrove heard the shower running and opened his eyes.

He sat up and squinted at the digital alarm beside the bed. 7:08. Too damned early for a Saturday morning. But since one of the sexiest women who had ever shared his bed was soaping herself down in the bathroom just fifteen feet away, he figured it was the perfect time to modify his schedule.

He got up and, ignoring the sudden nausea from too many vodka martinis the night before, crossed the bedroom, making his way for the bathroom.

Lana had already switched off the water by the time he stepped into the room, bleary-eyed, but just as erect and as ready for action as he had been just a few hours earlier. He had time only to watch the foggy shower door open and glimpse her wet, naked form filling the steamy doorway before she lowered her eyes and smiled. "I see Junior's up and ready for action again…"

"Nothing wrong with *those* eyes, is there?"

"Kind of early, though…" She grabbed a towel from the rack and began blotting her face. She regarded him for a moment. "I didn't think you were such an early riser." She smiled. "No pun intended."

"Clever." There was nothing better than a smoking hot babe who could keep up with him.

"Me? Or the pun?"

She was being a tease again. No biggie, especially since she was still obviously interested and eager to continue playing the game. He moved closer. It was going to be quite a while before he could gather up enough initiative to get dressed and drive her back to her car, which was parked behind the Katty Klub in South Orlando, where they'd hooked up the previous evening. "All that seems to matter to me this morning is the hot, naked babe standing in my bathroom, lathering me up again," he replied with a grin.

"I guess that's a good thing, then?"

"You're not very dumb, are ya?"

"No one's ever accused me of that." She bent over and applied the towel vigorously to her hair. The sight of her perfect ass proved too much, and he felt every bit of control vanishing quickly as he reached down to grab her hips and pull her smooth, warm flesh against him.

***

"Why don't you wanna talk about it?"

Lana's eyes stayed on Brent as she held a strip of bacon over her plate. Her face glistened from the morning sun drifting in through the kitchen blinds, settling on her and giving her thick black mane a bluish sheen.

He nearly spilled his coffee at her question. He knew what she was talking about; he just didn't want to spoil their breakfast by going into unpleasant details. This subject was upsetting; it couldn't possibly be considered pleasant breakfast conversation. "What are you referring to?" he

43

asked, hoping she could sense his obvious reluctance and tactfully shift her attention to some other less stressful topic.

She picked up her coffee cup. "Your accident—what else?"

So much for polite subtleties. There was no need to turn this into an argument. True, he didn't want to talk about it, but judging by her expression, she clearly wanted some explanation. Since this was their first date, he didn't see any reason to permit her to involve herself in his affairs. But since he wanted to spend more time with her, he decided to be as tolerant as possible. With a high-quality babe like her, a man had to make certain concessions. "What about it?"

"We all heard that you were involved in an accident. You were gone for several weeks, and then you came back. You seemed okay physically, but no one said anything about what actually happened, or where you were."

"And your question is…?"

"What happened?"

He shrugged. "I was in an accident."

She pushed out her lower lip in a fake pout. Under different circumstances, the action would have turned him on. But not now. It irritated him even more than her question. To compose himself, he visualized her naked once again. He was pleased that the anger vanished almost immediately.

"We already heard that detail," she replied. "I'd just like to know—"

"I was heading back home on Colonial and T-boned some woman in a Honda. That's it in a nutshell."

"One of the guys at work said you were drunk."

To play for time, he had more coffee. And, once again, to settle down. For some strange reason, the naked visual of her had suddenly stopped working.

The court case had stressed his alcohol consumption at the time of the accident. Knowing he couldn't possibly pass a field sobriety test, he'd refused to comply with the officer at the scene and was arrested and taken to the Station. Luckily, CF had enough horsepower to produce his bail and release him on bond. However, the next few days had been hell, explaining the situation to CF's lawyers and CEOs Richman and Garrity, who hated any modicum of negative publicity. He was then ordered to admit himself to a detox facility for ninety days. He hadn't spent the full ninety at the facility, passing by the skin of his teeth three weeks early before quietly returning to work. Dissatisfied with his decision, Richman and Garrity placed him on half days for the next full month.

"I'd had a couple," he told Lana.

She stared at him. A strip of bacon was trapped between her thumb and index finger. She appeared to be studying his expression. "You mean two?" she asked after a short silence.

"That's usually what a couple means," he said, growing even more uneasy. Her sudden frown was annoying. It suggested disbelief. "What bothers you about what I just said?"

45

"I've seen you drink, babe. I've been to half a dozen picnics and at least two parties since I started with CF."

"What's that supposed to mean?"

"I've never seen you stop at just two drinks."

He considered strangling her but decided it would be much less trouble if he just tried pacifying her—at least, for the moment. "All right, I might have had three, possibly four. But I wasn't *drunk*, dammit. I can hold my liquor. Even you should know that by now. You've never seen me fall flat on my face, have you?"

She ate the bacon, picked up a wedge of toast, and smeared it with strawberry jam. She bit into a corner, watching him as she chewed, then swallowed, washing it right down with coffee. "What happened to the woman you T-boned?"

His pulse began to hammer, and he felt the short hairs bristling on the back of his neck. Why the hell did she have to ask him that? Why was she putting him through this in the first place? Sure, she was gorgeous. Hell, she was a scorching-hot babe. But did a single night of mind-altering jungle sex with a chick who belonged on a Sports *Illustrated* cover justify discussing something he'd been trying to put out of his mind for the last three months? Why did *any* of it matter? It *happened*, for God's sake. The company bailed his ass out by paying off in a settlement. Everything should return to normal, right? He'd gone through rehab, and the woman he'd run into had been paid very well for her troubles. Case closed.

So why was this hot bitch bugging him about it?

"The company paid her off," he told her, and hoped she'd drop the subject.

"How badly was she hurt?"

He sat in tense silence, his blood simmering. What the hell was going on? Why was this babe asking so many damned questions?

After a minute or so, he decided that he had had enough and needed to find out where this nauseating third-degree was coming from. "Why do you wanna know all this?"

"Just curious."

"That's *all* this is? Curiosity?"

"I'd just like to understand what happened."

"But why?"

A shrug. "I'd like to know what's going on with a guy I'm messing up the sheets with."

"That's the *only* reason?"

"Why else would I wanna know?"

"That's what I've been trying to figure out."

"It's no biggie. Not really. If it bothers you *that* much—"

"Yeah. It does. It bothers me that much. It bothers me a whole shitload of that much. It bothers the tits off me!"

She regarded him in silence, looking both curious and concerned. Then she had another sip of coffee, put the cup back down and said, very seriously, "Brent...you don't *have* tits."

He couldn't help it; he laughed.

She smiled. "I'm glad I could snap you out of it."

"I was just a little sensitive. I still am, actually."

"I don't blame you."

"I blame myself, though."

"Do you?"

"Of course. I'd had too much to drink and shouldn't have been driving in the first place."

"But you didn't intentionally cause the accident, did you?"

"Of course not." Lana was right. He hadn't intentionally run into that Honda. He felt badly for what happened to the driver, that brown-haired babe he'd seen being pulled out of the car and placed on a gurney...but it wasn't like he'd been highballing it, was it? Just a light tap to the side, and with the help of an eyewitness, they'd proven that he wasn't doing much more than twenty at the time. Since then, he'd heard the babe hadn't been doing well, but once again, so what? It was an accident, and everyone knew that an accident was called that for a damned good reason. Accidents just *happened*. It wasn't planned, it just *happened*...

"It just happened," he said, struggling to convince himself once again.

"What?"

For a moment he had forgotten what they were talking about. "What the hell were we talking about?"

"You okay?"

"Of course. Why?"

"Just wondering."

"What the hell *were* we talking about?" Suddenly he wanted to know what had started all this.

"Your accident."

Her words caused his mind to go back there once again. *I need to stop this crap. I need to get her off this and coax her back into the bedroom. We can get it on once again so I can forget all about this.* "How's breakfast?"

She ate more toast. "You're a really great cook."

"You haven't finished your eggs."

"I'm getting to them. Why? Am I not eating fast enough?"

"Actually, no."

She blinked. "How fast should I be eating?"

"Faster than what you've been doing, obviously."

She finished her toast, picked up her fork, and scooped some scrambled egg onto it. She ate the forkful, then picked up her coffee. "You must be horny again."

"Ya think?"

49

Chapter 7

Owen opened his eyes and groaned.

The dog had slept on the bed with him. She lay on her right side, near the foot of the mattress. Her eyes were wide open. She was watching him as he stirred.

His first reaction was anger. He knew that it was misplaced, that he was only feeling it because the dog was lying where Morgan should be, and that he was deluding himself into thinking that Morgan would be lying there again one day. But as his mind cleared and he remembered the previous day, he realized that there was no reason in the world why he should be angry with this dog, and that her company, as unexpected as it was, had already succeeded in helping to heal some of his wounds.

"Sleep well?"

The dog blinked, sat up and yawned.

"I'm getting up now. Is that all right with you?"

No reaction.

Owen struggled out of bed and squirmed into his trousers. His guest watched him in silence.

"You can stay there if you want. But I've got things to do."

He went down the stairs to make coffee. He opened the fridge door and removed the packet of coffee. The moment he turned around, he discovered that the dog was watching him from the doorway.

"You decided to get out of bed. I guess that's a good thing, right? Or were you just lonesome?"

No reaction.

"Hungry?"

Silence.

"You won't mind if I make coffee, will you?" He held it up. "After all, I'm human. We can't function unless we've got half a gallon of coffee in our bloodstream before we leave the house. I'm sure that since you probably know all about humans, you already know this, but I'm telling you anyway. I don't usually talk to others about myself, but I've got this strange feeling that you just might wanna know a little about my day. Got all that?"

The dog raised her left ear a fraction and panted.

"I kind of figured you'd understand." He went over to the coffeepot. "It'll only take a minute."

The dog went over to the water dish. She lowered her snout to the bowl, made some impressive slurping sounds, then sat and watched him.

Owen made the coffee and put the packet back. He pulled out the package of shredded ham, grabbed a fistful, went over and dropped it into the dish for the dog. The dog got right up, sniffed the dish, then ate the ham. She had another slug of water, sat down, and watched him as before.

"You're welcome."

The dog seemed to smile.

"If you stay here, I'm gonna have to get you some actual dog food, you know..."

The dog snorted.

Owen shrugged. "It's like this. If I keep feeding you people food, you'll never get the nutrients you need from that lousy crap they ship over here from China."

Another snort.

"I hear ya." Owen sat down on the stool at the island and watched the dog as he waited for the coffee to brew.

***

Half an hour later, after he had showered, shaved, and dressed, Owen began wondering once again what he should do about the dog.

It was obvious that the animal belonged to someone. She was clean, well-behaved, and appeared to be in good health. Her teeth were white and in good shape, and she was alert and happy. Definite not a stray—which meant that there was probably an owner out there somewhere, looking for her. She wasn't wearing a collar, but that didn't necessarily mean she didn't belong to someone.

A chip.

Yes. If he was right, this dog was undoubtedly chipped.

This would require a visit to the nearest vet. One visit would be all it took to determine if the dog was wearing a chip. This would give them all the necessary information. Then he could quit worrying altogether and set about returning her to her legal owner.

But what if she *wasn't* chipped?

What would he do then? What *could* he do?

Worry about that when and if the time comes…

After brushing his teeth and combing his hair, he descended the stairs and went into the kitchen for another cup of coffee. The dog was sitting on the small oval rug near the water dish, watching him, her golden nub swishing quietly on the rug. The water dish was half empty. He filled a glass with fresh water and added it to her bowl. Her food bowl was also empty. He didn't want to overfeed her, so he left it empty. If he didn't have any luck at the vet's, he'd stop by the local grocery and buy her some high-quality dog food.

He wondered if he should tell her his plan. For one thing, he wasn't sure if she would understand. For another, he had no idea how she would react if she did understand. Either way, he felt the need to give her a heads up. He wasn't certain that she'd fully understand, but figured he owed her that much.

"I'm taking you to the vet."

The dog just yawned.

"I have to find out if you're chipped."

No reaction.

"If you're not chipped, you're coming back here with me. Will that be all right with you? Or would you prefer staying at the vet's while they try and find a suitable place for you?"

A short, soft "Woof..."

"Does that mean you're all right with coming back here?"

"Woof..."

"Does that mean you don't want to stay with the vet?"

No response.

For some reason he could not quite understand, he felt that the dog was somehow telling him in her own unique way that she approved of his plan. But just to make sure, he said, "Is this all right with you?"

Her nub twitched excitedly.

Owen grinned. "I may be totally off-base here, but I'm getting the distinct feeling that you're okay and on-board with what I just said."

Her nub continued to twitch.

"I guess we should just get this show on the road, then."

He poured more coffee into his cup. Then, just as he had another sip and went to grab his keys, an image of Broadway Avenue, where he had originally encountered the dog the night before, flashed in his head.

He stopped cold. Then he turned and stared at the animal. "Why am I suddenly thinking about that place again?"

The dog blinked.

"Did *you* do that?"

A slight flick of the nub.

"Does that mean yes?"

Another flick.

"Are you telling me that we need to go back there? Back where I found you? On Broadway Avenue? Just before I was about to use my gun on Hargrove?"

"Woof."

"Does this mean you'd like to go back there?"

The nub flicked again, this time more urgently.

"Is there a specific reason why you want to go back there?"

No reaction.

A sudden thought came to him, and he practically yelled at himself for not thinking of it sooner. "Does someone you know live there? Your people, maybe? The place where you live? Are you telling me you'd like to find your people?"

Silence.

"Are you just messing with me?"

Another flick of the nub.

"One last time. Do we go there? Or to see the vet?"

Yet another flick.

"The vet?"

No reaction.

"Back there, where I first saw you?"

"Woof..."

Owen shook his head. "I guess we're not going to the vet's, then."

Chapter 8

Lana Drake was sitting on the edge of the bed, fastening the straps of her high heels when Brent Hargrove stepped out of the shower.

He immediately felt the familiar stirrings and cursed himself once again for acting like a sixteen-year-old kid. *You're all grown up, for God's sake. If you can't control those cursed* cojones *by now, you might as well go back to high school.*

But it was tough. Lana was dynamite. He couldn't help himself for losing his nut every time he caught a glance of her velvety flesh or a whiff of her hair. And the fact that she had already turned down Garrity, Foss, and three top-notch investors did even more for his ego. Garrity was pushing sixty, but he was also worth eight mill, owned stock in a chain of condos, had a spacious riverfront mansion in Moss Park as well as a penthouse in Disney Village, and was part owner of one of the most prestigious golf courses in the Central Florida area.

Sighing deeply in satisfaction, Brent toweled himself off, applied the blow dryer to his hair, slipped on his bathrobe and went back out into the bedroom, where Lana was standing in front of the full-length mirror, forcing a hairbrush through that luxurious black mane.

Her tiny silver necklace lay on the bedside table, where she had left it. He stopped himself from mentioning it. He could remind her later—at work, perhaps. This, of course, might get her to come back for another visit.

He went right up to her, wrapped his arms around her waist and pressed firmly against her. And immediately felt his blood beginning to simmer.

"Don't muss me, now." She didn't miss a single stroke with the hairbrush.

"What's the problem? We're not on any sort of schedule, you know."

"I don't want to go out in public looking like I've just been laid."

"It's Saturday, girl. I thought we'd do the mall thing, then have lunch at Fashion Square before I drive you back to the bar to pick up your Camry."

"That sounds good." She squirmed free of him and went to put her hairbrush in her leather bag, which sat opened amongst the scattered pile of wrinkled sheets on the bed. She closed the bag and turned to face him. "You paying?"

"That depends."

"On what?"

He gave her a wink. "If I think you've been good or bad."

"You're silly." She grabbed her bag and slung the strap over her right shoulder.

"I've been told that before."

"I'll bet you've been told that a thousand times."

"You know me *so* well."

"C'mon, then." She headed for the open doorway. "You just promised me a few lovely hours at the mall."

57

He cringed. "A few *hours*?"

She turned around. "Of course. Then lunch."

He blinked. "A few *hours*? *Then* lunch?"

A smile. "Good. You're paying attention."

He couldn't believe what he could be getting into. He'd known several women who loved spending the entire day shopping and had dumped every single one of them. He'd just assumed Lana was different. At least, he'd *hoped* she was. But since the shopping issue hadn't been foremost on his mind, he hadn't been concerned about such details. "You're not one of *those*, are ya?"

"One of *those*?"

"A female who'd spend her entire existence in a store, if she was able to."

She smiled and batted her lashes. To him, an unbelievably bad omen. "That's me. Why? Is there a problem?"

"No. No. Hell, no. Not a problem." He made a mental note right then to have sex with her one more time before dumping her.

"You're sure?"

"Why'd you ask?"

"You've got this really painful look on your face."

"Indigestion."

"From breakfast?"

He sighed. It was pathetic to what lengths guys had to go for a piece of top-quality ass these days. "Sure. Let's go with that."

***

58

At just a few minutes before eleven, Lana got in the passenger seat of Brent Hargrove's Lexus and placed her bag on her lap.

Brent circled the car, opened the driver's door, and tried like hell to stay focused on getting the car started and not those gorgeous legs she was deliberately showing off just two feet away. Those same shapely limbs that had wrapped around his waist the night before. "Ready to go?"

She nodded.

He put on his harness, pulled the door shut, flicked on the ignition, put the car into reverse, then backed out of his spot.

As he was turning the wheel before proceeding up the drive, Lana said, "If you don't mind, I'd like to stop at the Post Office after lunch. I'm expecting a package."

He grinned. "Don't you mean *another* package?"

"Very funny."

"I usually get better later in the day."

"I should hope so."

"Ouch..."

"So...are you gonna stop at the Post Office or what?"

"No problem." He coasted up the drive and stopped at the curb. Traffic, as usual for Saturday, was heavy. He was about to turn right to pull onto Colonial when something caught his eye. He glanced to the right. It took him several seconds before the sight registered. Then he cringed.

About a hundred feet away, two figures were standing on the sidewalk on Colonial, watching him. A man and a dog. Although the dog didn't pique his interest, Brent clearly remembered the man. He was the husband of the woman he'd T-boned. The woman he'd sent to the hospital. The woman who, as far as he knew, remained in the hospital.

His heart thrashing, he stiffened, and his grip slipped on the wheel. His foot also slipped, sliding off the gas pedal.

The Lexus lurched forward.

A canary-yellow Smart Car heading east jerked to a sudden stop right behind him, but not quickly enough to swerve out of the way in time. The right-hand corner of its front bumper thumped into the rear panel of the Lexus, and a sickening crunch echoed loudly. The front of the Lexus jerked to the left, its bumper barely missing the westbound pickup zipping by.

Chapter 9

Owen Roth watched the chaos and struggled to determine what had just happened.

He glanced at his watch. It said 11:05. When they came here just minutes earlier, the same Lexus he had seen the night before inched its way up to the curb. And just moments later, it pulled out into heavy traffic.

Now it was parked alongside the curb, a sizeable dent in the rear panel.

Brent Hargrove was sitting behind the wheel, looking totally freaked as the growing crowd gathered around the scene.

His thoughts buzzed as he stared down at the dog. "Did you see that?" he asked, choking down the urge to laugh.

The dog's large brown eyes stayed fixed as she looked up at him. Her nub flicked briefly on the pavement.

"Does this have anything to do with that image I caught in the kitchen?"

The nub flicked again, just as briefly.

"Was this your idea?"

No response.

"I'm serious," he said, lowering his voice. "This is really baffling me. In fact, *you're* really baffling me. Tell me this has nothing to do with you. Please? Otherwise, I think I might just whip out my phone and schedule a quick session with the local psychiatrist—"

"Pretty dog," a woman said as she passed on the sidewalk.

"Thank you."

She stopped and smiled at the animal, then at Owen. She was about thirty, tall and extremely slender, and dressed in a tan business suit. Her features suggested she was Asian. Her thick black hair hung loose in a heavy curtain, shining brightly in the early afternoon sun. "Is it an Aussie?"

"I think so, yes."

"Does it bite?"

"I honestly don't think she does." He stared at the dog. "You don't bite, do you?"

The dog smiled and flicked its nub.

"I don't know her that well, but from what I've seen, she's very gentle." He shrugged. "She's quite the lady. I don't think she'd lower her standards and suddenly turn vicious."

The woman laughed. She bent, reached down and stroked the animal's neck. The dog smiled at her. "Her coat is so *soft*…"

"She came like that."

"And you're right, she does seem *extremely* gentle…"

"She seems to be."

The woman tilted her head. "Don't you know?"

"Well, to be honest…I just picked her up last night. I think she's a stray." He didn't know how else to say it.

"Well, she certainly seems to like you."

"I guess she feels sorry for me."

"Whatever works, right?"

"You got it."

The woman smiled. She said, "Have a nice day," then waved and walked away.

Owen turned back to the dog. "Are we finished here?"

"Woof..."

"Does that mean yes?"

"Woof..."

"Or does it mean no?"

No response.

"I guess this means we're no longer looking for your people..."

Silence.

"You didn't, by any chance, bring us here so we could *cause* what happened over there, did you?"

The dog's nub tapped the pavement.

"I'm hoping—I mean really and truly hoping—that your tail tap doesn't mean I'm right..."

No response.

"No, right?"

"Woof..."

He studied the animal's eyes. "I'm gonna consider the fact that you're just a dog, and not some sort of seer from a distant land and another time who has somehow assumed the form of a dog."

The dog cocked her head.

"I know, I know. I sound mental, right?" He shrugged. "I can't help it. I used to read a shitload of sci-fi when I was in college. Harlan Ellison, Sturgeon, Asimov, Bradbury—the works. Anyway, I sincerely hope you're a dog and nothing else. Otherwise, I'm gonna be too damned terrified to function."

No response.

"Nothing to say?"

Silence.

"So then, our next move is to head back home."

No response.

"I assume that's where you'd like to go. You haven't given me any hint as to where your people are, so I have no idea what to do about that."

The nub swished.

"But I really do need to stop at the grocery along the way and buy you some decent food."

The dog tilted her head.

"Okay with you?"

"Woof…"

"Okay, then."

Chapter 10

His mind in a daze, Brent Hargrove eased the Lexus closer to the curb, put the brake on and sat there, shaking, his head down, his eyes closed.

"Are you all right?" Lana asked softly, her hand touching his wrist.

Her touch was like ice. He pulled back, mashing his shoulder against the door. He was already disoriented, feeling like he had been stuffed in a box much too small and locked inside. His reaction, an explosion of raw emotions, rocked the inside of the car. "No, I'm *not* fucking all right, dammit!" He glared at her even though he could barely see her or anything else in his blind rage. "Do I *look* fucking all right?"

She pulled away and gawked at him, and he suddenly realized what he had done. Reality intervened, telling him he had reacted like a jerk, and that if he didn't fix this right now, things would quickly deteriorate. He took a deep breath and rubbed his eyes, then his temples. He let the back of his head fall against the seat. It relaxed him somewhat, at least for a few seconds, so he stayed like that while his thoughts spun wildly.

A man and a dog. They were standing right there, watching him. It would have been completely innocent if the man and his dog had been totally foreign to him. After all, this was Orlando, and everyone knew Orlando was chock-full of people wandering all over the place, many of them walking their dogs.

Nothing odd about a man and a dog interrupting their walk to stand there watching him, was there? Nothing odd at all…

Except for one major thing.

The man in question happened to be the husband of the woman he'd T-boned. The woman he had sent to the hospital.

This alone made everything very, very odd.

Why was the man there in the first place? Why was he standing right there on the sidewalk the moment Brent reached the curb and was about to pull out onto Colonial?

Were they the figures he saw the night before, when he was getting in his car to meet Lana at the club?

If so, why were they standing there? What the hell did the man want?

And why the hell did he keep bringing the damned dog with him?

Focus. Concentrate. And think. Push that damned panic away. Now, dammit! Before you do something equally stupid!

Where the hell do I start?

This one is easy. Start with Lana. She isn't the enemy, you idiot. She just spent the night with you. She's the only ally you've got right now. And you certainly don't want to do anything to piss her off or send her away…

He took another breath. "I'm sorry. I really am. I didn't mean to—I shouldn't have… This isn't…I really wasn't ready for this…"

She was still frowning, still gawking at him in a way that made him feel like he had just killed

66

someone. "Of course you weren't. It was an accident, wasn't it?"

He didn't reply.

"You didn't say what happened. Did your foot slip or something? You saw that car coming, didn't you?"

Then it dawned on him, and he suddenly felt even worse. He had no idea why in hell this happened. Or how it happened. He didn't even remember if his foot had slipped. Or why he pulled out when he did. Or why that Roth guy would be standing right there with his stupid dog the very moment Brent pulled up to the curb.

How long had he and the dog been standing there?

Most important of all: what the hell was in that guy's head?

Did he have an actual plan in mind? Was it this? *Causing* the accident? Was this what Roth had in mind all along? A revenge, of sorts? A sick brand of karma? To stand there and look him in the eye, which would shake Brent up enough to get him T-boned, just as Roth's wife had been?

This reasoning was ridiculous, and anyone with a working brain cell or two could probably figure out that what he seemed to be suggesting was way the hell out there in la-la land.

But how could he know for sure?

The answer came to him in an instant.

Go right out there and confront the son of a bitch...

67

His nerves jumped erratically as he straightened in the seat and gazed at the activity just beyond the windshield.

The sidewalk had quickly become crowded. People were congregated in assorted groups, watching the activity, while others inched slowly past in their vehicles, gawking.

The man and the dog were walking away.

"No! They *can't*—I've got to find *out* about this!" He struggled with the harness, clicking it open, and for precious seconds wrestled with it to break free. Lana said something to him, but he didn't hear her. He was much too busy trying to scramble out of the car.

By the time he pushed the door open and forced his way out onto the pavement, the crowd had grown, and he could no longer see any sign of the man who had caused all this. Brent tried pushing through the clots of gawkers, but just as he was about to reach the end of the snag, the loud, irritating whine of an approaching siren close behind him stopped him in his tracks.

***

"License and proof of insurance."

The cop stood outside the driver's door of the Lexus, looking impatient and disgusted. He was at least six-three and broad-shouldered, with large dark eyes, thick black brows, and a granite chin that looked like it had been chiseled by a sculptor who preferred square angles. His nametag said *ROLLINS*. His manner said, *I'm all business, so don't give me an attitude, and we'll get along.*

Brent pulled the cards from his wallet and handed them over. The cop marched back to his vehicle, which was parked alongside the curb, lights flashing.

Lana watched him in her side mirror. She turned to Brent and whispered, "He's not very nice."

He didn't reply. He was much too busy wondering what the hell had just happened. And yelling at himself once again for fucking up the beautiful car he bought just three months ago—brand-new, right out of the damned showroom. And, most of all, trying—and failing—to determine the motivation of the man who had somehow caused all this.

The man who was now gone.

The bastard and the damned dog were walking away right after I pulled over and parked...

That was what he observed.

Was this some sort of payback? Did Roth think that by doing this, Brent would suffer in some way for what he did to the man's wife? That hexing him would make him atone—at least financially—for the pain and suffering Brent had caused the woman?

He immediately scolded himself for thinking such absurd thoughts. He realized more than ever that he was thinking of things only someone with serious mental issues would come up with. A revenge-obsessed man showing up at the precise time Brent was pulling out onto Colonial? Hoping Brent would freak? And wreck his expensive new car? And cause a major traffic snag?

69

How the hell did Roth even know Brent would be pulling out when he did?

Impossible. And silly. And as stupid as anything he had ever considered before.

"You never said why you did that," Lana said suddenly, interrupting his growing inner madness.

"Did what?"

"Pulling out into passing traffic. I thought you were a good driver."

He said nothing. He had no idea what he should tell her because everything he was considering would make him sound totally whacko.

"Does this have anything to do with your accident?" she asked. "The one that happened three months ago?"

Her question made him wonder why she even mentioned it. Did she actually *know* what was going on in his head? How *could* she? She didn't know him very well. Aside from half a dozen innocent flirtations at the office, they were strangers working at the same company. This was their first date, and except for the wild, mind-blowing sex they'd enjoyed during the last twelve hours, they really hadn't engaged in any serious, meaningful conversation.

What could she have heard at the office that he hadn't told her? That the woman he T-boned was rushed to the hospital and put in Intensive Care? That Brent had gone to Garrity and Richman and begged them to buy his way out of a potentially devastating lawsuit?

Now she wanted to know why he had caused this fiasco, and he had nothing he could tell her that

70

would make any sense. He couldn't tell her that the husband of the woman he'd sent to Intensive Care had been the cause of this. Or that the husband was standing on the sidewalk, waiting for him as Brent brought his car up to the curb. Or that this man would walk away once Brent had involved himself in another accident.

What *was* all this? What the hell was happening?

And why did he suddenly have the strong suspicion that he was beginning to go stark raving mad?

The cop came back and handed him a slip of paper. He said something about what was on the paper, and that Brent should sign it, and something else that said that Brent had been cited for the accident and should appear in court a certain time from now, and that he could contest this if he was represented by an attorney...

He wasn't paying attention. He was much too busy trying not to feel sorry for himself. He signed his name, but the moment the cop took the paper away and marched back to his cruiser, Brent immediately began zoning out again...

Chapter 11

After the dog jumped into the Challenger, Owen slid in behind the wheel, pulled the door shut, and tried once again to figure out what the hell just happened.

An image of the street half a block down from the Parkway Towers apartment complex flashed in his head.

I drove here, got out of the car, took the dog out, started walking down the street, and then—

Hargrove pulled out and was immediately sideswiped.

Very strange.

Had Hargrove been freaked out or distracted?

Had he been drunk? At this time of day?

Would the idiot get into an expensive new car after hitting the bottle and brave lunch hour traffic?

He suddenly remembered the woman sitting in the front seat beside Hargrove. An extremely attractive young woman with thick black hair.

Hargrove, as he recalled, was not married. From what Owen had learned through the lawsuit and from court records, Hargrove was some sort of investment broker who'd been working at CF Investments for the last ten years. The man dressed well and lived well, and the fact that he owned a penthouse suite at his young age conveyed the clear message that he had money and knew how to spend it.

Owen guessed that the woman with Hargrove was either a girlfriend or a date.

Judging by the girl's appearance, Owen decided that Hargrove could have indeed been distracted while he was driving.

Owen struggled to recall other details. Although much of what happened had become a blur, he clearly remembered Hargrove gazing at him from behind the wheel of the Lexus an instant before the accident.

This, of course, made Owen wonder yet again why he had come here in the first place.

Was it because of the dog? The fact that he thought the image blip had come from the animal? That it had something to do with his locating her people? Her home?

Was this somehow her frantic attempt to return to the scene in a last-ditch effort to reconnect with the people who might have dumped her?

Or was this something else? Something much too weird for him to comprehend?

This didn't make any sense. He was thinking about taking the dog to the vet to determine if she was chipped. However, he drove here because an image of this street flashed in his head.

But why did he have to be here to see Hargrove pulling out in heavy traffic only to be sideswiped by a passing vehicle?

Did the dog somehow cause this?

Frustrated, confused and a bit frightened, Owen slipped the key into the ignition slot. Then, sighing tiredly, he sat back. The dog sat stiffly, staring at the chocolate-brown SUV parked in the spot directly in front of them. It was clearly obvious that the animal seemed lost in thought.

A dog lost in thought.

Am I freaking out? Going out of my mind?

The evidence seemed clear. This beautiful animal had strangely entered his life and seemed to be communicating with him in a way he would have never suspected.

What was she trying to tell him?

And why had she suddenly come into his life?

Chapter 12

After Lana slipped into the Mall, Brent Hargrove stayed outside, glaring at the damaged Lexus.

Even at the relatively low speed it had been going, the Smart Car had done quite a number on Brent's luxury ride. A corner of the Smart Car's bumper had mashed into the side panel of the Lexus at a forty-five-degree angle, peeling off a healthy strip of silver at least two inches wide, burrowing down to bare metal and replacing it with a sickening two-foot-long yellow string an inch thick at one end and pitted on the opposite end.

He wanted to spit blood. He bought the car three months ago and had put less than twelve hundred miles on it. It had been immaculate from the moment he drove it out of the showroom. Now it looked like just any other expensive ride with a big ugly nasty smearing it. The damage would probably run close to five K—no matter *who* he took it to.

But the part that really ripped into his gut was that the car could never ever be *immaculate* or *new* again.

"God*dammit*!" The urge remained, but now he also wanted to destroy the stupid jerk that had done this. The asshole driving the Smart Car. And also that other asshole, who had distracted him just enough to cause him to lose his concentration and let this happen. And all because of that damned accident three months earlier…

The woman's name was Morgan Roth. Brent remembered it clearly. He couldn't remember her husband's first name, but that wouldn't be difficult to track down. As an investor, he boasted valuable sources of information all over town. Besides, CF's CEO George Richman had a cousin or niece working at OPD. One or two phone calls would be all it took to get Roth's full name and address.

It was important to find out why Roth had been standing there in the first place, even more important to find out why he and that stupid dog had disappeared the moment after the accident.

"Bastard," he said under his breath, "I don't know what you have in mind, but you're definitely fucking with the wrong—"

"Fender bender?" asked a high-pitched voice just a few feet behind him.

Startled and enraged by the interruption, Brent spun around.

A skinny kid around twenty or so in cutoffs, a ragged *MAGIC* tee shirt, and black flip flops stood just a few yards away, hands on hips, grinning stupidly at him. His *DOLPHINS* cap sat sideways on his head, the brim turned far to the right, making him look dim-witted.

Brent didn't know what had lit him up more— the grin, the cap, the hairy feet, or the ridiculous question. It really didn't matter much at all. The interruption had ignited a fire in his gut, and before he realized it, he had stomped right over. At six-one, he was nearly half a head taller than the boy and probably forty pounds heavier. But that didn't matter much, either. Right now, he was hot and ready for bear. However, he fully understood that getting into it with a kid in a public parking lot would most likely cost him his job and his career, and that he should do whatever was necessary to control the rage building up within him. It took every fiber of his being to refrain from calling this shithead every name in the book, grabbing him by the scruff of the neck, slamming him to the pavement, jumping on him and pounding his face into mush. But when the reality of the situation cleared his head, what came out of his mouth was, "*What* was that?"

The kid shrugged. "Just a question, man. Cool ride. Pricey, too. Shame you got it all fucked up."

Despite his efforts, the urge swept over him and took over completely. Before he realized it, he had grabbed the kid by the neck of his tee shirt and pulled him close. His right hand had already formed into a fist and his arm was pulled back, ready to break free. He was about to slam his fist into the punk's idiot face when a familiar voice a fair distance away yelled, "*Brent! Don't!*"

Blinking away some of the rage, he turned.

Lana was standing at the top of the steps near the front entrance, her eyes wide open, her hands up, covering her mouth. Even from that distance he could see she was trembling.

At that same instant, the fury within him had dissolved, and he realized what he had nearly done. With a heavy sigh, he let go of the teen's tee shirt, dropped his arm to his side and stepped back.

"D-Dude? What the *fuck*?" The kid's face had turned white. His eyes filled the sockets, and he was shaking. "You fuckin' *nuts*?"

A wash of cold drifted down Brent's back, and he found that he was also shaking. He couldn't look at the boy; all he could do was stare at the filthy pavement at his feet. There were six mashed cigarette butts, a gum wrapper, and tire marks over what resembled a crushed candy bar. He also saw the kid's flip flops as well as his feet. And when rationality nudged him again, he knew he needed to resolve this. His mind just wouldn't cooperate. All he could think of to say was, "Get lost."

The kid was already running away, the loud flapping sound of his flip flops diminishing quickly.

Brent slowly raised his head.

Lana was now standing just a few feet away, glaring at him. "What the hell is going on with you?"

He wanted to say something, but nothing would come. He couldn't even remember what had happened and began trembling when all he could see was darkness. He rubbed his temples, closed his eyes, and tried to force himself to recall what he had done. An image of the battered Lexus quickly appeared, and the events of the last few minutes automatically followed. "That kid," he said to Lana in a harsh whisper, "he…he pissed me off."

Her eyes grew as she watched him. "Really? And you were about to *kill* him?"

Not knowing how to reply, he just nodded.

"What did he do?"

"Nothing."

78

"What did he say?"

He struggled to remember. It didn't come right away, but after a minute or so, the cursed words tore into his head, bringing it all back. In a trembling voice he said, "Fender bender.'"

Lana blinked. "*Fender* bender?"

He nodded.

Her expression convinced him she thought he was clearly out of his mind. Then she took a deep breath, collected herself and said, "In other words, that boy looked at your car, said, "fender bender," and you decided to *kill* him for that?"

Coming from her, the kid's words seemed innocent enough, but at the time, they burned like flame. As he stared into Lana's shimmering green eyes, he suddenly realized that nothing he could say would accurately convey what had been happening to him. His world was coming unglued and there didn't seem to be anything he could do to change things.

"Well?" She was obviously waiting for a reply.

The fact that she was growing impatient, plus the contemptuous expression on her face, infuriated him. A searing wave of hatred and betrayal swept heavily through him. He had just spent the previous night making love to this beautiful young woman, for God's sake. Things should not end up like this. Not at all. The two of them should be feeling some sort of bond, some connection. She should be supportive of him. Sympathetic. Understanding. She had seen what happened to his car, how it had affected him.

But she was demonstrating none of these reactions. It made him feel humiliated, abandoned. Tossed aside, like yesterday's trash.

"*Talk* to me, Brent!" Still standing there, her hands on her hips, her eyes blazing. Waiting for some sort of explanation. Some justification.

"He just pissed me off at the wrong time, and I wasn't in the mood."

He wasn't surprised at all when she groaned, shook her head and said, "You're sick, Brent. Really and truly sick. And don't bother with me from now on. I mean it. I'll get a damned cab." Then she dropped her hands, spun on her heel, and stomped back toward the front entrance of the Mall.

Chapter 13

Sitting behind the wheel of the Challenger, Owen turned to the dog.

"I really need to know why I suddenly had the urge to drive out here," he said. "I may be totally off-base, but I clearly remember getting the distinct impression that I might be able to get you back with your people if I brought you back."

The dog yawned.

"Was I wrong about all this?" He shrugged. "I'm kinda new at this dog-whispering shtick, you know."

Silence. The animal still seemed totally unimpressed by the situation.

Owen decided that it was time to approach this from a different angle. "Was that image I saw coming from you? The one about us driving back here?"

No response.

"What were you actually trying to tell me?"

Silence. The dog licked her paw.

"It didn't work, did it? Even if your people are out here, the crowd and the pandemonium caused by the accident made things slightly more difficult."

The dog yawned once again.

"Am I boring you?"

No response.

"All we did was freak out that asshole into causing an accident and messing up his new car."

The dog's nub swished on the seat.

"That *was* kind of entertaining, wasn't it?" Owen couldn't help grinning.

Another yawn by the dog.

He sat back and tried analyzing things again but knew he could come up with nothing that would explain this. There was no reason in the world why he should have come back here. This area was entirely too busy and congested to go about looking for the owner of a dog. It was commercial, with shops, churches, and offices everywhere. And as usual, the tourists cluttering the highways made things even more hectic.

So now that he realized what a boneheaded move that was, what was his next option?

The vet's, obviously.

At least that made more sense. This way, he could try to locate the owner by using technology, rather than gut instinct—which turned out to be a complete bust.

"We're going to the vet," he told the dog. "And I don't want to hear another word about it, understand?"

No response.

"I've really got no choice. I've got to find out who you belong to, don't I?"

Her nub swished on the seat.

"I can't just take you back to my place if you belong to someone else, you know…"

Silence.

"That's called dognapping. And I can get slapped with a hefty fine for doing it."

The dog blinked.

82

"I like you and all, but I really don't want to treat you as my own dog if you belong to someone else. One of these days, someone is bound to see you, and by that time, I'll probably be really stuck on you. That's probably because you're really easy to get stuck on, and also because I kinda think it's already happened. But it'll only make things worse because the cops'll show up one day, put a collar on you, take you away, then slap me with a damned fine."

No reaction.

He groaned. "This doesn't bother you at all, does it?"

The dog's left ear twitched.

"All right, then. If you're not gonna add anything constructive to the conversation, I guess I need to shut up and take you to see the vet."

His mind made up, he flicked on the ignition, put the car in gear and eased out of the parking space.

Chapter 14

Instead of driving back to his penthouse suite, Brent Hargrove headed to the nearest bar.

After the fight with Lana, as well as the confrontation with the stupid teen punk, he needed to unwind.

The Bottoms Up Bar 'n Grill, on North Semoran Boulevard, was already packed and rowdy with the lunch crowd by 1:15, when he parked the Lexus in the side lot and went inside.

He climbed a stool near the doorway and didn't waste any time ordering a double vodka rocks from the skinny brunette babe the moment she hurried over.

The juke was playing something hip-hop, but the crowd was so loud that it drowned out the selection. The bargirl brought his drink right over. He slipped her a twenty, told her to keep the change, then downed half the drink in one swallow. It did the trick, warming his insides and relaxing his nerves. He closed his eyes and let the magic happen. And while the anger and the frustration ebbed quietly away, he began thinking of how his life had been unraveling in just the last couple of hours.

He recalled the night before, when the two figures were standing across the street as he went down the aisle in the parking lot to get into the Lexus.

Were the figures Roth and the dog he saw this morning? Or was he just imagining things because the accident had shattered his mental state and made him paranoid?

He drained his drink and signaled the bargirl for another round. In the meantime, he began to wonder what he should do about all this.

Was there some sort of fix possible? And if so, what was it? A confrontation? Should he demand what Roth was doing outside the apartment complex the very moment Brent had left with Lana to take her to the Mall?

His blood began to boil once again.

The dark image of Lana marching back into the Mall made him grind his teeth. She hadn't sympathized with him at all and had completely ignored his feelings. She hadn't seen—nor even cared—what he'd been going through. Instead, she condemned him for his frustrations, his anger, his lashing out. She had freaked out by his outrage, then turned her back on him. Her expression told him that he was no longer someone she wanted to deal with. And when she turned and hurried away, he realized he was dead to her from that point on.

Yes, something had to be done about this. He had no intention of letting the bastard Roth ruin his life.

What the hell was this, anyway? Payback for putting Roth's wife in the hospital? As he had told the lawyers and the cops, it was an accident. He didn't know the chick from Adam. Hell, his Lexus was worth at least two times the price of the damned Honda the chick had been driving. How could anyone think this was intentional? He hadn't even been going that fast in the first place. If he had been crazy enough—or drunk enough—to want to do serious damage, he would have been going much faster than what they'd estimated. Sure, he had a few, but he'd driven with a higher alcohol content hundreds of times before and, with the exception of a couple of minor mishaps years ago, managed to survive without too much trouble.

An *accident*, dammit. A fucking *accident*!

The bargirl brought him another drink. He handed her another twenty, picked up the glass and sucked down half of it while thinking about what he could do to turn the tables on the asshole who seemed intent on wrecking his life.

Chapter 15

The scan took just seconds.

"Anything interesting?" Owen asked.

"No chip." The thin, dark-haired tech frowned. Her nametag said *Renee*. She was around thirty and had large dark eyes and thick, long lashes. Her thick, curly black hair was tied in a tight bun. She looked Hispanic.

"Why the frown?" He sensed a problem.

The tech carefully studied the scanner. "Something's not working right."

"Something wrong with the scanner?"

"Either that, or the chip was absorbed. But I think it's the scanner. Can't see anything in the display." She took the instrument over to the counter near the sink and laid it on a silver tray.

"What would cause that?"

"With technology?" The tech chuckled. "Anything's possible."

"Or nothing…"

"Exactly. But it's kind of an old scanner, so…"

"Technology aside…a beautiful animal like this one should be chipped—don't you think?"

"You're not very familiar with dog owners, are ya?"

"I know most of them are stupid and ignorant, and don't know how to care for a dog. Many of them let their pets roam free. Others don't even bring their pets with them when they move to another state. Still others drop their dog off at the Humane Society after the wife delivers a kid and doesn't want to worry about the dog hurting the kid. Yeah, I know a little about dog owners."

"Then you know a lot of things happen that shouldn't."

"Yes."

She looked at the animal and suddenly seemed confused. "You say you just found her?"

He smiled. "Actually, I think you could say she found *me*..."

"You're lucky, then."

"Lucky?"

She smiled at the dog, who sat there, looking up at Owen. "She's pretty, well-mannered, gentle, didn't try to bite me, and obviously worships you. That says a lot."

"*Worships* me?"

"She hasn't taken her eyes off you since you brought her into this room."

The dog swished her nub the instant his attention focused on her. "She does seem to like me, now that you've mentioned it."

"It wouldn't take a genius to figure that one out."

He turned back to the dog. "Is this lady right? Do you really worship me?"

The dog's nub swished furiously. She replied, "Woof!"

The tech laughed. "I guess she just told you what you needed to hear."

"I guess she did at that."

The tech suddenly turned solemn. She arched a thin black brow. "Now *please* don't tell me you're gonna take her to the pound."

"This dog ain't going anywhere, lady." He couldn't believe she said such a thing.

"Woof!"

The tech laughed. "All righty, then. Now you can tell me you're gonna want her chipped."

He gazed at her, then at the dog, who was still watching him intently. Once again, he thought about the dog's owners, then decided that if they really cared about the animal, they would have had her chipped. "You wanna wear a chip?"

No response.

"I guess she doesn't."

"She probably just doesn't understand," the tech replied.

"Maybe I should try and find out something about her owners first."

"Woof!"

The tech laughed. "Well, she certainly understands *that*."

He laughed. "I guess we've both decided not to get that chip right now."

***

On his way back to the apartment, Owen stopped at the supermarket.

He turned to the dog. "I'm only gonna be a couple of minutes."

The dog blinked and began to pout.

Owen felt himself beginning to soften and wondered if this beautiful animal had indeed been dropped off. "I'm coming back…"

The dog's nub swished a few times, but her large brown eyes stayed on him.

"I have to get you some decent food, but I'm coming right back. I promise."

The dog seemed to relax.

"Listen. I have to come back to pick up my car. I don't intend on walking home, you know. It's quite a few miles to the apartment and kind of hot out there. Besides, I'm pushing forty, and don't like walking too much anymore."

"Woof."

He left the motor running with the a/c on, got out and hurried into the store.

Fifteen minutes later, he left the store, opened the back door, and set the bag with ten pounds of dry food, a dozen cans of expensive, high-quality dog food, and assorted treats on the seat.

He slid in behind the wheel. "I told you I'd be back, didn't I?"

The dog stood up in the seat. Her nub flicked furiously. She whispered, "woof," then lowered back into the seat and rested her left front paw gently on his thigh.

Smiling, Owen instinctively placed his hand over the dog's paw. The animal whined. He felt her warmth taking over, relaxing him. This was a dog, after all. He'd owned dogs before. His parents had also owned dogs.

What was different about this one?

Everything, he heard himself thinking.

Like what? that other voice asked.

I don't know. But somehow, this dog is different.

How?

For one thing, she's helping me heal.

90

Really?

Yes.

How else is she different?

Her touch.

What about it?

It feels...different, somehow...

Different how?

I don't know. All I can say is that, well, she doesn't seem like a dog.

What does she seem like?

I don't know how else to say it, but almost...spiritual...

Pulling himself back to reality, he put the car into drive. Just then, an image blipped brightly in his head, and he had another strong urge to drive back to the Parkway Towers.

The vision of the accident came right back, and he told himself he didn't want to go back there ever again.

But for some reason he could not possibly understand, he felt the irresistible urge to return to the damned place.

Chapter 16

"Slumming, Mr. Hargrove? I figured you for the Disney Village scene. Or maybe Church Street."

Randy Samuels, a salesman at the Lexus dealership on West Colonial, had been dealing with Brent's car purchases for the last three years. Samuels was barely thirty, but for the last couple of years had earned a solid reputation in the business of selling luxury cars. He was small, about five-six, and weighed no more than one-thirty. His slicked-back, moussed black hair and small dark eyes made him look like a gang member. Brent always thought Samuels could have earned a spot as a small-time street thug in a *Law & Order* episode, or *Blue Bloods*. Samuels set his beer bottle down on the counter and opened the first two buttons of his shirt over his red checkered tie, which had already been pulled down a couple of inches.

"On your lunch break?" Brent asked.

Samuels checked his wristwatch. "More or less."

"How do your bosses feel about your clubbing it before getting back to the old grind?"

Samuels laughed and picked up his beer. "Fuck 'em," he said, grinning. "Besides, all they seem to care about is how many cars I'm selling. And believe me, I sell a shitload of 'em." He jabbed a thumb toward the front door. "What happened to the Lex? That's yours out there near the door, right?"

Brent nodded and had another sip of vodka.

Samuels shook his head. "What the fuck happened? I just sold ya that babe not so long ago."

"I got sideswiped just before lunch."

"Today?"

"Yep."

"Whose fault was it?"

He sighed tiredly. "Mine." He wanted to go into detail but didn't want to get angry all over again.

"Where'd this happen?"

"Outside my apartment complex on Colonial. I was pulling onto the main stretch when my foot slipped, and a fucking Smart Car rammed into my side."

"Ouch."

"That's one way of putting it..."

Samuels had another slug of beer and thought it over. "Why'd your foot slip?" He glanced at Brent's glass. "Were ya...I mean, did ya have a couple?"

A wave of anger flared, but he fought it back down.

Samuels shrugged. "I just asked 'cause it didn't sound like something you'd do. That babe's eighty K, ya know."

"I know. I signed the fucking papers."

"Were ya distracted, maybe?"

Suddenly he wanted to move away from the crowded bar. An empty table showed at the other end of the large, hazy room. He got up, picked up his glass, and gestured for Samuels to join him.

Right after they sat, Brent said, "I guess you could say I was freaked out. That was what caused the accident."

93

"Freaked out?"

He decided to give the man a condensed—as well as sanitized—version of the incident. He didn't want to come off sounding like the guilty one. He knew that he was but didn't want to look like a schmuck. He figured he'd fudge the numbers a little to get it all out. He thought that doing so might make him feel better.

"There's this guy. I kinda had a disagreement with his wife, and he decided to come after me to toss a sizeable bunch of shit at me."

"What kind of disagreement was it? This a sex thing? Or did it have anything to do with that accident you were in before you came back to the dealership, couple months ago?"

Brent nodded, a little pissed that Samuels had figured it out so quickly.

"What I heard was, you put a lady in the hospital."

Brent finished his drink and signaled for a refill. *Keep your cool. You don't want a repeat of what happened with that stupid kid outside the Mall.*

"Her husband…he tried to even the score," he said evasively.

"How?" Samuels asked.

The brunette came to his table with a refill. She took his twenty and empty glass, then hurried back to the bar.

"He distracted me while I was pulling out onto Colonial."

Samuels nodded reflectively and had another slug of his beer. "I can see how that would fuck you up."

"Well, it did, and if I'm not mistaken, he's probably gonna do something like that again."

Samuels' eyes grew. "What makes ya think so?"

Brent had a sip of his fresh drink. He decided to fudge even more with this tale of bullshit. He lowered his glass. "The bastard told me he was gonna do it."

Chapter 17

As he left the supermarket parking lot and drove back to Colonial, Owen struggled to comprehend what his sense of logic had been telling him.

It sounded not only weird, but also something that had caused him to fear that he might be losing his sanity.

Once again, the images showing up in his head had told him to go back to Hargrove's apartment complex.

He just could not find any justification that would explain this puzzling need to return. He didn't want to be anywhere near Hargrove and would have preferred not to live in the same county with the same firm of shysters that had manipulated the scales of justice to prevent the man who had recklessly put Morgan into a coma from being hauled off to prison.

His body stiffened and turned cold as the familiar horror unraveled once again in his head. Everything thundered back in one cold, dark flash. The accident. The phone call. The frantic trip to the hospital. The image of Morgan lying helplessly in her hospital bed.

And, of course, the official, unemotional "apology" sent to him via special messenger by Hargrove's fleet of attorneys, as well as the sizeable check for his "compensation," and another generous check to cover Morgan's medical expenses. And, to add insult to injury, the well-prepared written "apology" sent by Hargrove himself.

And lastly, yesterday evening, standing outside Hargrove's apartment complex, the .45 centered on the bastard's forehead only moments before the dog interrupted his plan of ultimate vengeance.

His hands tightened around the wheel and quickly turned numb.

Although he had originally wanted to hate the dog for her interruption, he realized how ridiculous that reaction really was. And even though her sudden intrusion had destroyed his mission to rid the world of Hargrove, he fully realized he couldn't blame this innocent animal for anything. She was a dog, plain and simple. Dogs didn't operate on the same level as people. She was merely looking for someone to help her find her way. The fact that she had somehow picked him seemed immaterial. And even though he had had other plans at the time, he knew he had to step up.

"Any reason why we keep coming back here?" he asked as he stopped at the red light one block west of Hargrove's apartment building.

Her only response was a sudden flick of her nub.

"Nothing?"

The dog merely watched him.

"Does this have anything to do with finding your people?"

No reaction.

"You don't want to give me any sort of hint— or sign—that tells me your people live around here?"

The dog yawned.

"Are you telling me this was my idea? Coming back here? Not yours?"

"Woof..."

His pulse fluttered. "Does that mean yes?"

No response.

"No?"

Silence.

"You realize, of course, that even if we do find someone who knows where you come from, explaining why I haven't told the cops about you is gonna make me look like a moron."

More silence.

He glanced at the dog and grimaced. "I still don't know why I haven't done that, you know..."

The animal smiled at him.

"Yeah. You're right. I do know. For once, I'm glad you *can't* talk. Calling me a sucker might just piss me off a little more than I'd like right now."

"Woof..."

"Uh-huh. I get it. But what I *don't* get is why we're here again. And I don't think you're about to tell me, either."

No response.

"No comment?"

Silence.

"Not even the tiniest hint?"

Another yawn.

This was getting him nowhere. "Doesn't this seem stupid to you?"

The dog's nub swished.

He nodded. "Yeah," he said. "It really is."

The light turned green. He proceeded straight, heading east.

A minute later, he turned onto Broadway, pulled over to the curb and parked. As he switched off the ignition, he discovered that his right hand had already moved over to the comfortable padding of the console lid, which contained the revolver.

Chapter 18

Slightly drunk, Brent Hargrove sat slumped behind the wheel of the Lexus outside Bottoms Up Bar 'n Grill, gazing stupidly at the number on the card Randy Samuels had given him.

It was the phone number of a man Samuels knew. A friend. A buddy who did odd jobs for friends and acquaintances. A dude who would do anything for the right amount of money.

The card said, simply, *Tom Blocker.* A phone number was printed below the name—nothing else.

Should he or shouldn't he?

What the hell did Samuels say about this guy? Something about this Blocker dude doing whatever needed to be done? Something about him being a little crazy, but that he was efficient as hell? And a seriously tough dude as well?

Brent sat back and let his thoughts go wild. Every instinct in his being told him not to go along with this. This sort of thing not only sounded bad, it also felt bad. Blocker was obviously trouble. Getting involved with someone like him, someone who did anything for money, could be the worst decision he might possibly make.

Would it be worth it?

Samuels was an okay guy for a car salesman. As a hustler, he did what they all were noted for. Lying. Stretching the truth. Making all sorts of insane promises. Distorting things.

Could these people be trusted? Brent knew damned well that no one in his right mind could trust anyone who peddled cars for a living. None of them were much of a visible cut above politics or the law profession, and every single one of them would sell his own mother for a price. They could tell you the sky was green and would be so damned convincing, you would feel guilty if you didn't believe it.

In other words, could anyone with more than two or three functioning braincells trust any one of them enough to go with such a referral? A recommendation involving a man who would do anything for money? A man who could handle something seriously sensitive without getting the cops or the homicide squad involved?

What exactly had he told Samuels in the bar?

Even in his half-drunken state, he clearly recalled the details of their conversation.

"Her husband obviously wants to even the score," he told the man. And when Samuels asked more about it, Brent said, "He distracted me while I was pulling out onto Colonial."

And then Samuels had said, "I can see how this kinda shit would fuck ya up."

To that, Brent had said, "Well, it did, and if I'm not mistaken, he's probably gonna do something like that again."

Samuels thought that over. Then he frowned and said, "Whaddya wanna happen here? You want someone to scare this dude? Make him leave you alone? Or do ya want him to go away permanently?"

Permanently. The word slapped him squarely in the face. It hurt, and he had to admit that it also

101

knocked him for a loop. Most important of all, it made him think, and after just a few minutes of weighing the pros and the cons, he reluctantly reached the conclusion that he had no idea what to do about this.

When he told the other man his feelings, Samuels said, "How 'bout if I get a buddy of mine to take care of this quietly? If it's done right, this asshole freaking you out will think twice about bothering you again."

Brent hadn't liked the tone of that. It sounded like something you'd expect to hear in one of those Mafia movies.

I gave him an offer he couldn't refuse...

"Tell me what you mean by quietly," he replied, hoping his paranoia was making more of this than what he had initially feared.

Samuels had a slug of beer. He put the bottle down and looked Brent in the eye. "Here's how I see it. This guy who's been freaking you out... You must admit that he's got a pretty damned good reason for doing this, right? I mean, you did mess up his wife."

Brent sighed tiredly and drained his drink. Samuels at least had *that* right. Yes, he did mess up Roth's wife. Putting her in the hospital could definitely be classified as messing her up— especially since after three months, she remained in the hospital. "But I didn't mean it!" he quickly added, slamming the empty glass on the table.

"That doesn't matter," Samuels replied flatly. "Not to that guy. Deliberate or not, his lady's in the hospital. She's not at home with him, cooking his meals, talking to him, getting him laid, sitting with him in the living room each night, watching Netflix or Hulu, or sharing the sheets with him later on. What you did or did not mean to do just doesn't cut it. Not in this case. You messed her up, and that's all this dude cares about."

"All right, dammit. I messed her up. We both seem to agree on that. So then, what's next?"

"What's next is up to you."

"What the hell does *that* mean?"

"Simply this. Do you just want him to stop the harassment shit before something worse happens? Or do you want him messed up just like his wife?"

Chapter 19

For nearly an hour, Owen Roth sat in the Challenger, fighting the strong urge to take the Smith .45 out of the console.

I need to do this, he kept telling himself. *If I don't, I probably won't be able to live with myself.*

Maybe, came the wretched voice inside him that continued ruining his plans. *But now is not the time.*

Why not now?

Does it feel like the right time?

No. It didn't. In fact, it never felt as wrong as it did at that precise moment. But why? Why was he suddenly so reluctant now? Just hours ago, he could think of nothing more satisfying than emptying his gun into Hargrove's skull.

Why did it feel so wrong now?

Was it because of the dog?

He told himself that this had nothing to do with her. In fact, the more he thought of it, the more he realized that his reluctance to grab the gun had not been influenced in any way by the dog.

Then what *was* the answer?

The main reason was that he could not see Hargrove's car in the lot. It was that simple. And, as anyone with normal intelligence could figure out, walking around carrying a gun on constantly monitored private grounds was probably the stupidest thing anyone could possibly do.

Yes. It was stupid. And even though he could think of nothing else that would make him feel better, he had to face the reality of the situation and come to terms with the negatives in this scenario.

Too many variables, for one thing. What if he missed? What if he didn't miss, but Hargrove managed to survive? What if someone saw him?

And what about the monitors?

His conscience was right. This was indeed stupid.

It certainly *wasn't* the right time, after all.

Sighing tiredly, he sat back in his seat and tried to decide what he should do.

A few minutes later, at nearly four o'clock, he glanced to his left and stiffened.

Hargrove's silver Lexus appeared amongst the heavy traffic just up ahead and began slowing down. Its signals blinking, the vehicle turned left in the break in traffic before easing down the inclined drive that led to the front lot facing the apartment complex.

The moment Owen spotted the Lexus, he felt his thoughts explode into a sea of hot red, and all the variables that had made him change his mind earlier immediately vanished.

"There he is," he whispered tensely, more to himself than to the dog. "And just when I was convinced my mind was made up."

The dog merely yawned.

He took a few deep breaths and forced himself to chill. This was no time to lose his cool. This could prove to be the opportunity he missed the night before. The important thing was that he knew exactly where Hargrove was and had an excellent idea of where he would be for the time it would take to get out of the Challenger and enter the building.

He tried to relax but quickly found that he couldn't. He didn't want to sit here like an idiot and wait for something to happen. He was sick and tired of delaying the inevitable.

But he knew he couldn't just pull the revolver out of the console, get out of the car and get this done. He couldn't—not with the dog sitting there right beside him.

But he couldn't remain here, either. This was pointless. He had to do something about this, but he had no idea what that something could possibly be.

What about the dog? Drop her off somewhere?

Take her in to OPD and hope one of the cops was a dog lover?

He had already considered that option and shot it down. Taking this animal into the police station and leaving her was something that would haunt him for the rest of his days, even if this day turned out to be his last.

What other options, if any, were there to consider?

He had to think more about this. And then he had to reason it out, and this time stick with his decision—whatever the hell it was.

Chapter 20

"Is this Tom Blocker?"

"I go by Tug. But yeah, I'm the one and only. Who's this?"

"I'm a friend of Randy's."

"Samuels?"

"Yes. I've been buying cars from him for the last couple of years."

Another pause. "You Hargrove?"

Brent pulled the cell away from his ear and gawked at it. How did this guy know about him when he and Samuels had just been talking less than half an hour ago?

His nerves twitched as he slowly brought the phone back to his ear. "I'm Brent Hargrove. How'd you know—"

"I just got a call from Randy about five minutes ago."

That made sense. But it also made Brent a little suspicious. "What exactly did he tell you?"

"Just that you might be calling me to do a job."

"Nothing else?"

"He also said some asshole's been followin' you around."

Brent sighed. "That's about what it amounts to."

"Well? Interested in what I think ya want done here?"

"What do you think I want done?"

"Nothin' over the phone, get it? You can never tell—know what I mean?"

"Copy that."

"We'll discuss the other stuff later on, after I fix this for ya."

Brent didn't like the sound of that. *Fix* was such a scary word nowadays. It sounded permanent. "Fix?"

"You don't want him chasin' after ya anymore, right?"

"Yes, but—"

"But what?"

"I really need to get this settled first. I mean, between us. I don't want—"

"Listen. How 'bout I call ya right back?"

"Why would you want to do that?"

"I'll use a different phone."

"A burner?"

"Ya got it."

"Sounds good."

"Gimme a sec." *Click.*

Fix. Want done. No matter how he looked at it, he feared that this man might be a little too heavy-handed to resolve this.

His cell buzzed. It was Tug. "All righty, now. Just tell me you're not gonna be tapin' any of this on your end."

"That would be stupid. Don't you agree?"

"Sure do. But ya can't tell what people are gonna do anymore. They're, well, fuckin' crazy."

"That's a fact. But you have my word. Now I'd like you to tell me you'll do what I ask."

"That's what I do. Otherwise, people start flappin' their gums and no one trusts me anymore."

"Sounds reasonable."

"Okay, then. How's five hundred sound?"

"Five hundred?"

"It's my goin' price."

"Just what're you gonna do about this guy?"

"Whatever ya like. Unless you want him to disappear for good. For that, I gotta handle this thing a much different way, and I'll have a shitload of expenses…"

He didn't like the sound of that at all. It was bad enough that Roth's wife was still in the hospital; he didn't want to have Roth killed just because the man had been acting out of grief, or hysteria. Contract murder was seriously bad. He didn't want to do anything that would shitcan his future. "I just want him to stop bugging me. Scaring him would probably work. Do you know how to scare people?"

A short chuckle. "Hell, I've been scarin' people half my life."

"How?"

"I never reveal my methods, okay? This way, you're clean."

"Copy that." He figured Blocker might have to hurt Roth to get him to understand, but some people had to learn things the hard way. Especially people who weren't in their right mind.

"At least we got *that* outa the way…"

"Now all we have to do is find out the man. I'd hate to have to ask anyone where he lives. That'll undoubtedly raise some eyebrows, won't it? And I can't very well do an online search. Everyone knows that once you're on the Net, you've no longer got any privacy. It would help quite a bit if—"

"You got a description?"

"I'd say he's around my age, which is thirty-five or so. He's about six feet tall and broad-shouldered, with dark-brown hair cut kind of short, and last I saw him, he was wearing jeans and a maroon short-sleeved shirt."

"Does he have a dog with him?"

Brent felt his body go tense. How the hell did he know about the dog? "Yes. As a matter of fact—"

"A brown and white Aussie-looking mutt? Maybe fifty, sixty pounds?"

"H-How did you know—"

"I've seen both of 'em."

"Where?"

"Right now, they're on Broadway Avenue, directly west of your apartment building."

Brent's hackles immediately went up. How the hell did this Blocker guy know where he lived? "How do you know—"

"I just told ya I was talkin' to Samuels."

"That's right." He let out a deep sigh. "I guess I'm just a little nervous about all this."

"Just chill. It'll turn out all right."

"I hope so…" Brent rubbed the back of his neck. "You did say this man's on Broadway right now?"

"I've been watchin' a guy and the dog walkin' around. He got on Colonial, then came back and let the mutt sniff around and then piss on one of the bushes."

"Can you tell what he's doing now?"

"Sittin' in a gray Challenger."

Brent found this unbelievable. It sounded much too easy. Much too convenient. "You're sure that's him? Right there? This minute?"

"Unless he left in the last couple minutes. If he's plannin' on messin' with ya, he's probably still there."

"That certainly makes things simpler."

"Couldn't be easier."

"You sure you can handle this?"

"Piece of cake. I'm parked less than two minutes away."

"Then this shouldn't take very long…"

"Not long at all."

"Hope it turns out okay."

"Don't worry about it. I've done stuff like this before."

"There's no problem, then. Is there?"

"What else you talkin' about?"

"What if the dog tries to bite you?"

"If I get bit, do I gotta tell ya what happens?"

"Just don't put yourself in a situation where you'll be vulnerable. Dog bites get recorded."

"That shouldn't be an issue. I don't wanna get bit, so I'll be careful."

"Good."

"Ever get bit by a dog?"

"No…"

"Well, just in case you haven't figured it out yet, it hurts like a motherfucker."

"I can imagine."

"If it's bad enough, you end up havin' to get a fuckin' shot. And if the damn thing's got rabies—"

"I get it, okay?" Brent was getting tired of talking and wanted this to be over. "Do what you have to do. Just try not to make it messy, all right?"

"In case you haven't already figured it out, I don't do messy."

"Good."

"I hit hard, though. I don't like to spend too much time doing something that shouldn't take longer than just a few minutes to get done."

He nearly groaned. This Blocker guy really did sound rough. Maybe too rough. "Just get it done, okay? But don't kill the guy. And try not to kill the dog if you don't have to. You know how upset people get when they see a dead dog."

"Okay, okay… You're the one handling the money."

"Just so you know."

"You'll hear from me shortly." *Click*.

Brent pocketed the cell phone. Then he went over to the portable bar in the living room and grabbed the vodka bottle.

Chapter 21

While his canine companion squatted near a bush, Owen watched the steady traffic zipping down Colonial.

His mind began to wander, and he found himself slipping back into time. Incredibly, many of the compacts whizzing by could have been Morgan's Honda. A couple of times, he thought he pictured his wife sitting behind the wheel. He had to remind himself that he had completely zoned out but decided instead to remain in the safety of his memory, recalling a pleasant time in their past, a time when Morgan had—

Shaking himself back to the present, he rubbed his moist eyes. When his vision cleared, he noticed a shadow close beside him. He looked down.

It was the dog. She looked sad.

Stop this right now. You're giving off something unpleasant and she's picking up on it.

He sighed and forced a smile. "I'm okay now."

"Woof."

He kept his eyes on her as they returned to the Challenger. He had been reluctant to let her out of the car fifteen minutes or so earlier because he had no leash, but for some strange reason, she had shown no sign of running away. He decided to let her walk around a little. She trotted along beside him, sniffing the sidewalk before settling on one of the bushes lining the path. Then hurried back and kept close.

Once she jumped in the passenger seat, he got in, closed the door, and spent the next few minutes gazing nervously at the console, where he kept the gun. As he stared, he found that he no longer wanted to bring the gun with him when he went inside the building. He began experiencing a strange repulsion and felt himself pulling away from the console.

The dog was watching him intently but gave no response.

His heart raced in his struggle to understand what was happening to him. His first thought was that this dog could read his mind, but he quickly discounted that observation as absurd. As far as he knew, that would be impossible. He had heard and read things about dogs and their remarkable abilities...but reading minds? That was just a tad over the top.

You're losing your perspective...

He was letting this animal freak him out. And as a result, he was no longer able to concentrate.

Was this because the dog had already upset his plan to kill Hargrove? Or did all this have something to do with Hargrove's recent fender bender?

This animal is doing a job on you.

Why couldn't he think clearly anymore? Why was he turning every single aspect of his life into total confusion?

He had to stop agonizing over this. It was doing him no good, for one thing, and was distracting him, for another. He had to clear his mind and get it back to what he was thinking before. It took him a few moments, but he finally remembered what his focus had been. He had to figure out what he had to do with this dog, and he had to figure it out as soon as possible.

Just then, an image of someone moving in his direction blipped in his head.

He turned.

A big guy was crossing the street and coming straight for them. As Owen watched, he realized that the man hadn't taken his eyes off them. He wore a sweatshirt, jeans and tennis shoes and walked briskly as he made his way directly to the Challenger. He appeared to be at least six feet tall, broad-shouldered, and well over two hundred pounds. He also looked young—on the right side of thirty. An expression of intense determination covered his dark features as he expertly dodged traffic.

What bothered Owen most of all was that this guy's right hand was buried in the side pocket of his jeans.

Chapter 22

As he approached the Challenger, Tom "Tug" Blocker kept his right hand buried in his pocket, firmly grasping the compact Ruger six-shot auto.

The gun was tiny, but amazingly accurate even with its two-finger grip. Hopefully, he wouldn't have to use it. Tug's size and muscle were usually more than enough to intimidate the average dickhead. But if he did need to use the gun, it would do the job and would be extremely easy to dump. A gun you can hide in the palm of your hand can be tossed anywhere.

But it probably wouldn't be necessary to bring firepower into play. Judging by what Hargrove wanted, just a few well-chosen words would be enough. Most stalkers freaked once they realized they were being watched. They almost always made for the hills when confronted by a six-foot-two weightlifter who had played football in high school. The mixed martial arts that came later on didn't hurt, either, if the target tried being a hero.

In this case, a dog was in the picture, suggesting that this might turn out to be a tad more difficult. Dogs tended to get in the way during a messy confrontation.

"Try not to kill the dog if you really don't have to..."

Sure, sure. But if it looked like he was about to get bitten, the dog would have to be put down. Tug had no intention of sacrificing a finger or anything else for the sake of a lousy five-hundred-dollar, ten-minute gig.

He decided to approach the Challenger from the driver's side. This way, he'd be clear of the dog and out of range. If the asshole wanted to get rough, grabbing him would pose no problem. Pressing the barrel of the gun to the dude's head would be all that was needed to take care of Hargrove's problem.

If the dog objected, he was just gonna have to cap the damn thing. He didn't really go for that option, but he knew damn well that shooting the dog just might get the driver to cooperate.

His adrenaline beginning to heat up, Tug marched right up to the driver's door. Using the large knuckles of his left hand while tightly gripping the Ruger with his right, he rapped roughly on the window.

The window immediately slid down quietly.

He bent down, so his face was less than a foot away, and quickly put on his patented mean expression. He expected the unmistakable look of panic to register on the man's face.

However, what he saw was something much different.

Chapter 23

Owen already had the .45 out of the console and wedged behind his back by the time he rolled down the window. He was about to ask what the big guy wanted when the dog began growling softly.

He hadn't taken his eyes off the figure standing outside. The young guy was not only big, but he also looked powerful. He was obviously the bully type, one who was no stranger to fights. Several long, jagged scars showed whitely on his forehead and jaw, and his nose had been broken, possibly more than once.

It didn't take a genius to realize that this guy had not come over to ask for directions, or spare change.

He had to consider the strong possibility that this might be a carjacking.

Owen cautiously tightened his grip on the .45. He decided that the casual approach might work in this case. "Is there a problem?"

The young man was watching the dog. His small blue eyes had opened wide and suddenly looked dazed. A moment later, fear showed on his face, and he pulled his head back. He began shaking. His gaze hadn't left the dog. Then, in a soft, throaty whisper, he said, "That your dog?"

Owen could tell the kid was stalling. "You could say that."

The stranger nodded but didn't reply.

Owen was getting impatient and wanted this business over with. He didn't want to shoot the kid,

118

but he also didn't want to just sit there and wait to see where this went. "Is that why you came over? To ask me about my dog?"

The kid frowned and looked confused. "I really don't know…what…I'm doin' here…"

Owen wondered if this could be a drug issue. He didn't see any glossiness in the eyes, but the boy seemed nervous. Owen had some experience with weed in college. Although he hadn't smoked in nearly fifteen years, he clearly remembered the signs. The shakiness was there, but the eyes were not blood-shot, and the boy wasn't acting goofy or dim-witted. Owen could not smell booze on the kid. But *some*thing was wrong, and even though Owen no longer felt threatened, he knew he shouldn't let down his guard. He said, "You're the one who came over and rapped on my window."

The man continued gazing at the dog. His face paled, and the expression of fear in his eyes intensified.

"Maybe you should go right back where you came from." Owen kept his grip on the .45 and edged it an inch or so away from his back to release some of the tension just in case he needed to pull it out in a hurry.

The young man didn't reply right off. After another pause, he said in a soft, unsteady voice, "Uh, thanks. Maybe I will. I think I will. Yeah…I think I'll do that…" His gaze remained on the dog as he straightened. Then he turned and walked back to the main highway. Despite the traffic, he kept walking, this time at a leisurely pace. A blaring of horns echoed sharply, and traffic from both lanes stopped abruptly to avoid hitting him. He crossed the street, went west for about a block, turned right, and disappeared between buildings.

Owen watched until he could no longer see him. He couldn't help noticing how the young man had moved much differently. When he first approached, he had moved more quickly, more deliberately, giving one the impression that he was ready for action. But when he left, he strolled slowly and unsteadily—as if he'd been drinking. The moment he was halfway across the street, his right hand emerged from his pocket.

Owen rolled the window back up and put the revolver back in the console. "What the hell was that all about?" he asked, looking at the dog.

The dog stared back at him. Her nub swished the seat.

"Why do you think he came over here?"

The dog blinked.

"There are parked cars everywhere in this area. You have any idea why he picked us?"

The dog whined softly.

Owen studied her expression. The concerned look in her eyes told him she might have been aware of something strange.

"If you know, would you find some way of telling me?"

A tiny whine.

He stared at her, trying desperately to read her expression. Although her body language told him nothing, he had the oddest feeling that this animal knew what was going on.

120

Chapter 24

The sounds of honking horns brought Tug Blocker out of a strange fog.

He shook himself and realized he was standing in the middle of the street, surrounded by traffic. He quickly sidestepped out of the way and slipped past two parked cars.

What the fuck happened?

Why did he feel like he'd just come out of a sound sleep?

He made it to the end of the block, turned right and walked over to where his car, the two-year-old black SUV, was parked in the gravel lot behind the office building. He climbed in, pulled the door shut, flicked on the ignition, turned the a/c on full blast and let it blow directly on his face, cooling him off and getting rid of some of the sweat that had covered his forehead and cheeks in the last few minutes. Once he started feeling more like himself, his brain began working again.

The dog.

The way it had looked at him…

And that growl…

That was all he could think of right now. That quiet, deadly growl. And the soft voice…

It was the voice of a woman, but it seemed to come from the dog. Yet he knew it couldn't be coming from the dog because that was impossible. How could a woman's voice come from a dog? How could anything sounding human come from a dog?

But he heard it, nonetheless. The voice of a woman, and it said: *"You should be ashamed of yourself…"*

Ashamed of yourself…

And in that next split second, he saw—or *thought* he saw—the face of a woman directly above the dog's head. The face was that of a beautiful lady with red hair and green eyes, and she was staring directly at him…

And then, in the next instant, the face was gone, and he was gazing at the dog's big brown eyes again, thinking about the woman's face and her voice, and before he realized what was happening, he knew that the voice had been right, that he really and truly should be ashamed of himself.

The dog's eyes focused on him, this time even more deeply than before, staying there the longest time before drifting into his soul…

His soul…

That was what had torn into him. It was the dog as well as the woman and her voice, and yeah, he knew full well that somehow they could see inside him. His thoughts. His feelings. His spirit. What had made him what he was today. It took him back…all the way back to his youth. And one of the first things he remembered was that half-drunk dude he'd beaten half to death in high school eight years earlier, when the team had won the title game, and everyone had gone to the Fire Hall down the street from the field to celebrate their victory. And that arrogant punk that had walked right up to him and told him he looked like a pussy and that he didn't have the balls to stand up to a six-year-old. That same pile of shit that, just five minutes later, lay whimpering in the alley behind the big block building, his face cut up and so bloody that he was unrecognizable, his eyes swollen shut so badly that he couldn't see Tug Blocker standing over him, watching him sobbing softly into unconsciousness.

Then there was that dirty insurance salesman who had been bleeding Tug's parents dry. The bastard who had suffered that nasty accident when he went into the men's room in the Bank Building on Robinson Avenue after cashing some sizeable checks. That arrogant jerk who, after some intense persuading, courtesy of Tug's huge square knuckles, had promised to issue Tug's parents a hefty refund check as he knelt in front of a urinal, his swollen, bruised face mashed to the bottom of the flow, his bloody mouth pressed firmly against the soaked urinal cake…

And the dickhead employing a bogus investment scheme to steal from one of Tug's high school friends…

And the cokehead tormenting one of Tug's childhood sweethearts…

Too many to count.

The important thing was that Tug had been squeezing bad, unscrupulous people, threatening them, beating them up and humiliating them for the last seven years.

But now, as he slouched behind the wheel of the SUV, the a/c blowing full in his face, he thought it frightening that one look into a strange dog's eyes would bring everything back. Every single damned thing he had ever done to another human being.

123

Every bleak episode that had happened in his twenty-six years on this earth and was stored permanently in the darkest, most secret recesses of his brain.

That was what had brought it all back. The redheaded woman and her voice, for one thing. And then that single look into the dog's eyes that had made Tug Blocker realize that a very, very dark, twisted soul existed in his body. A shadowy, tormented spirit that would never ever see the light of day—at least not in *this* life.

"You should be ashamed of yourself..."

And when all this horror finally registered, he lowered his head slowly. While resting his forehead on the steering wheel, Tug Blocker closed his eyes and began to sob quietly.

Chapter 25

Owen quickly discovered that his recent encounter with the big guy had prompted him to re-evaluate his thinking.

Had Hargrove been responsible?

If so, what was the motive?

True, it wasn't much of an encounter—just a few words   before the intruder turned around and walked away.

Once again, Owen wondered if the boy had been tripping. He had the strange feeling that the guy had been in some sort of trance. It seemed even more apparent when Owen suggested he leave.

"Uh, thanks. Maybe I will. I think I will..."

Had he been tripping?

Or was something else going on?

If Hargrove had been behind this, why did the boy walk away without so much as a threat, or even some mild chest-thumping?

This caused Owen to do some intense soul-searching. If that bit of business had been some sort of threat, he thought that maybe he should leave before something else happened. If Hargrove's intent was to call in someone to scare him off, Owen needed to be ready for whatever happened next. Sure, the encounter hadn't amounted to anything, but that didn't mean there wouldn't be others, did it? And if Hargrove had indeed wanted Owen out of his space, he might just find the right muscle the next time.

It was time to leave.

He was getting ready to pull out of their space when something very strange occurred to him. Stiffening, he put the car in park and sat back. And stared at the traffic passing by. Then he turned to the dog.

She sat up in the seat, looking straight ahead, not moving. Her tongue hung out of her mouth. She seemed to be listening.

He wondered what was going on in her head. He had questions he needed answered but had to remind himself yet again that she was a dog. And even if she did have some idea of what was going on, she couldn't very well tell him, could she?

She suddenly raised her head and turned to him.

A clear image of Brent Hargrove flashed from the picture screen in his head.

Taking a deep breath, he waited for his pulse to settle down. "Did *you* just do that?"

The animal displayed no response.

"That picture I just got in my head. Hargrove. Did *you* just send it to me?"

The dog blinked once and swished her nub on the seat.

"Does that mean yes?"

The dog's left ear twitched.

"That ear thing…did *that* mean yes?"

A tiny, almost inaudible whine.

"That whine… Was *that* a yes? Or do you have to pee again?"

Another swish of the nub.

"You're not gonna make this easy, are you?"

"Woof…"

126

"I guess I'm too stupid to figure this out by myself, right?"

"Woof..."

He tried even harder to read her expression. Despite his efforts, he just couldn't interpret her silence. "I'm going out on a limb and will assume that your "woof" meant "yes." You have any problems with that?"

The dog's nub swished eagerly.

"I'm gonna count that as a yes as well."

No response.

"One last question. If that was you behind that latest image, does this mean I need to see the bastard? I mean personally? Face to face?"

The dog stared at him a few moments, then replied, "Woof."

"You do understand that the big guy who just came to see us might have been sent by Hargrove, don'tcha?"

Another "woof."

"That doesn't matter to you?"

Silence.

"Does it matter that if I do get close enough to the bastard to actually touch him, I might try and kill him?"

"Woof." The dog's eyes did not waver.

"You're telling me you think I should do this anyway? Talk to him—not shoot him? Just ask if he'd sent that kid? And also to let him know that I'm not gonna do anything to him?"

"Woof." The animal smiled.

Owen shrugged. If there was indeed a reason to bring this ugly matter to a head, the dog's responses were making it crystal clear. "All righty, then. I guess this means I'd better do what I'm supposed to do, right?"

Her nub swished once again.

128

Chapter 26

Brent Hargrove's cell buzzed.

His nerves quivered the moment he saw the number. He hadn't seen it before but had a good idea who it was. And since less than an hour had passed from the time he talked to Blocker, Brent was almost one hundred percent sure that this guy was calling him back to give him a progress report.

The cell buzzed again.

His pulse pounding, he cleared his throat and pressed *talk*. "Yes?"

A slight pause. "Know who this is?"

"Of course. Did you see him?"

Another pause. "You could say that."

"Well? How'd it go?"

This pause lasted much longer, making Brent slightly uneasy.

Blocker finally said, "Not exactly the way I wanted it to go."

Brent felt his heart sputter. "What the hell does *that* mean?"

"Well, it's like this…" The man went silent.

"Hello? You still there?"

"I'm here."

"I'm waiting..."

No reply.

"I'm still waiting, dammit."

The man sighed. "Listen, Mr. Hargrove…I really don't know how to say this, but—"

"Just tell me what happened."

"I'm not sure I can."

"Let's take it one step at a time."

He heard another sigh. But the man still didn't speak.

Brent took a breath and struggled to stay calm. "All right, then. Just tell me this. Did you see the man?"

"You asked me that before."

"I'm asking again."

"Yeah, I saw him…"

So far, so good… "Did you approach him?"

"You could say that…"

Brent didn't care for that reply. It reeked of distraction and, worse, failure. "Speak plainly, all right? Did you or didn't you approach the man?"

"Yeah."

"Did you speak to him?"

A pause. "Yeah. And no."

Brent gripped the phone tighter. "And what the hell does *that* mean?"

Another pause. "This is where I guess you could say everything went sideways."

Brent struggled to understand what the man was trying to say. It was important that he heard more of the story. But since Blocker was being evasive, Brent would have to urge things along. "I told you to speak plainly, dammit."

"I'm *tryin'* to."

"All right, then. Let me ask you again. Did you or did you not speak to the man?"

"Like I just said, yeah. And—"

"To repeat myself, what the hell does that *mean*?"

"It's like this. I approached the dude's car."

130

"That sounds good—especially since you couldn't possibly have done anything if you *hadn't* approached the car."

"Well, that's what I did."

"What happened after that?"

A heavy sigh. "This is where everything fucked up."

"How?"

"I rapped on the window and your guy rolled it down."

"Okay…"

Silence.

"I'm waiting…"

More silence.

"Keep going. What happened after the window rolled down?"

"I don't…actually know…what happened after…after that."

"What?"

"I just said—"

"I know what you said. I'm right here, listening to you. I just don't believe you."

"I don't believe me, either."

"Then why don't you just try telling me what happened once Roth rolled down the window?"

"Everything got, well, sorta foggy."

"Foggy?"

"Yeah."

"What *sort* of foggy?"

"Whaddya mean? Foggy's foggy."

"I mean, was he doing anything? Drugs? Did you smell anything funky on him or coming from the interior of the car?"

"No..."

"Then you need to explain to me what you mean by—"

"Once he rolled down the window, the dog sitting in the seat beside him growled...and things sorta went...well, dark."

"Dark?"

"Dark."

"Are you trying to say you blacked out?"

"Maybe..."

"Whaddya mean, maybe?"

"I mean I don't *know*, dammit! As I said, *things went dark!*"

Brent didn't know what to make of any of this. Blocker was either hallucinating or he'd been doing hard drugs. Samuels hadn't mentioned if Blocker was a dopehead. Brent just assumed that the man's friend would be sober enough to do what he was to be paid to do. But this was weird. The man had actually *blacked out* when he'd first laid eyes on the dog.

"What exactly did you mean when you said things...*went dark?*"

"I don't *know* what I mean or what the fuck happened. One moment, I was starin' at the dog. Then I was crossin' the street, headin' back to my car."

"And you didn't say anything to Roth? Anything at all?"

"That's just it. I *don't remember!*"

This was incredible.

Blocker had blacked out. He'd rapped on the window, and when Roth rolled it down, Blocker

132

looked at the dog sitting beside Roth, heard the mutt growl, then blacked out.

How the hell could something like this happen? Blocker was lying—that much was obvious. But why?

It didn't matter, did it? Why he was lying was immaterial. The important thing—the *only* thing— was that he hadn't fulfilled his promise, hadn't done his job.

Which left Brent Hargrove with the same problem he had before.

Roth was still out there.

Chapter 27

Before getting out of the Challenger, Owen began thinking once again about his decision to confront Hargrove.

He realized that he no longer felt the overwhelming urge to kill the man. He didn't know if it was because of the dog or because he was just getting tired of the whole sordid business. Morgan remained in a coma, but she was still alive, and until her condition changed, he didn't see the point in committing suicide or spending the rest of his life in prison for murder.

Was this new mindset in any way prompted by the big guy who had approached the car?

He realized right then that the only way to view the complete picture was to ask Hargrove if he had indeed sent the young brute to scare him.

Would a simple visit to see Hargrove clear all this up? Or would it make the situation worse?

What if Hargrove *hadn't* sent the kid? What if the kid had singled out Owen for a carjacking and had been scared off by the dog? If this were the case, Hargrove certainly wouldn't know anything about the encounter.

Is this what had happened? Or had Owen been right all along about Hargrove sending the brute?

He turned to the dog, who was still watching him. "You realize how confused I am about all this, don't you?"

The dog blinked.

"Why should I waste my time trying to talk to him? What if that kid *hadn't* been sent by him? What if Hargrove has no idea what just happened?"

No response.

"What if he answers the door and I suddenly realize that I have this overwhelming urge to wrap my hands around his throat and choke him to death?"

Again, no reaction.

"You're not making this easy, you know..."

A tiny, almost inaudible whine.

"Whining just ain't gonna cut it. Not in this case, anyway."

"Woof..."

"That's a good start. A tad more information would be greatly appreciated."

No response.

"My gut tells me you understand every damned word I'm saying."

The dog's nub tapped the seat.

"In other words, I kinda think I'm right about you."

No response.

"Nothing to add?"

Silence.

"You mean I'm all alone in this?"

The animal lowered her head and placed her right paw on his thigh.

Owen felt his heart warming up once again. "Don't get me wrong. That's very nice of you. That paw thing? It helps, especially since I've been going through this nightmare with Morgan."

The dog didn't move.

"But this issue with Hargrove… It's tearing me apart."

A soft whine.

"I just don't know if talking to him will accomplish anything. I honestly don't think an idiot like him would tell me if he had actually sent that big brute to threaten me."

Silence.

What if he had?

What if Hargrove really had sent the big lug to do some structural damage to your good looks?

Before realizing it, the very idea of the situation had turned his thoughts red. He groaned deeply and shook his head. The rage came back, and he found himself trembling in anger.

The dog sighed softly.

"Let's stop all this damned mental crap and get this show in the road." Careful of her paw, he pulled open the console lid and grabbed the gun.

The dog eyed the revolver as he pulled it out.

"Something on your mind?"

Her eyes didn't budge from the gun in his hand.

"Let me try a wild guess here. You don't want me taking this with me."

A soft whine.

"What if Hargrove has a gun?"

The dog blinked.

"I know he's a Wall Street type and all, lives in a penthouse and spends a fortune on his hair, nails, and clothes…but he could still own a gun. He might even know how to shoot the damned thing."

Another soft whine.

"You'll feel awfully bad if he shoots me, you know. Especially since I left the gun in the car because you made me feel guilty about bringing it."

The dog continued staring.

"I've been planning this for months, dammit. I've dreamed about it, for God's sake. Hargrove deserves this. Trust me, he really does. He put my lady in the hospital, and it doesn't look like she'll ever come out of it." The rage continued surging inside him.

The dog tilted her head and whined softly. She looked sad.

"I don't want you arguing with me. I have to face that idiot right now, while everything's burning away in my soul. I don't want you messing up my plans by looking at me that way." He was gazing intently at her as his hand gripped the cold metal of the revolver.

The metal abruptly turned warm, then hot. Gasping, he let it fall back into its niche. He stared at it for a while, then raised his head and gazed at the dog. For some strange reason, she didn't seem at all surprised by what had just occurred. He gawked at the revolver again. Nothing different there, but he couldn't deny what had just happened.

He swallowed a lump in his throat. "Did *you* do that?"

The dog blinked.

"How the hell—"

The animal lowered her head and yawned.

His mind went crazy as he thought about it. How the hell could this dog—

137

Simply impossible. Sure, the dog seemed very perceptive and all, but could she actually stare at a gun and make it—

No. Not likely. No matter what happened, this dog did *not* make that happen. She couldn't have done anything like that. She was a *dog*, for God's sake.

But he could not ignore the distinct look of intelligence and understanding in those big brown eyes.

"Are you trying to tell me you don't want me to use that gun?"

A tiny, almost inaudible whine.

The back of Owen's neck tingled. Was he imagining all this?

Once again, those eyes stayed on him.

"Was that a yes?"

Another whine.

Still watching her, Owen quickly went through his plan once again. Grabbing the gun. Crossing the street. Taking the elevator up to Hargrove's floor. Pressing the buzzer. Waiting for the door to open, then putting several slugs into the bastard's face—

Then what?

Coming back here? Acting like none of this ever happened?

Or doing the sensible thing by saving that last bullet for himself?

What would happen then?

What would happen to this dog? Would anyone notice her sitting here while the cops and the medical guys were busy taking his corpse to the morgue? It would take the cops and the crime unit people considerable time to go through his wallet, find his address, drive to his condo, investigate, and then start hunting down the Challenger. This could take hours, perhaps all night. And this dog would still be sitting here in a hot car, waiting—

And waiting.

He couldn't leave her here. "You're making me feel like a stupid idiot, you know."

The dog's nub swished.

"You know I can't leave you here while I do this, don't you?"

A tiny whine.

After more thought, he said, "You've been trying to steer me away from killing him all along, haven't you?"

"Woof..."

"Dammit."

Another swish of her nub.

"You think I should just talk to the son of a bitch instead of blowing his brains out?"

"Woof."

Owen continued staring at her. Was this really about the dog? Or was his own conscience finally stepping in, giving him the clear picture he had never seen before? What was so different now? How could this animal have changed everything in such a short time?

How could she have taken the rage from him so easily and made him feel as if the worst thing he could do was kill the man responsible?

"How the hell are you doing this? How could you change my mind about all this in just one day? Morgan's lying in a coma, and everyone at the hospital has been bugging me about having her tubes turned off. My life has become a shambles. I have nothing to live for, and—"

A tiny whine.

"I've wanted him dead for *three months*, now…"

Her nub tapped the seat.

"But now, because of you, I suddenly have this strange feeling that I might not want to kill him at all."

She blinked.

"You're a real pain—did you know that?"

No response.

"I've been planning to kill that jerk since the day Morgan was taken into Intensive Care. Now you come into my life, and I suddenly don't want to kill him at all. I don't want to kill him because that would mean you'd be trapped in this hot car until someone discovered you, and I couldn't *ever* go along with something like that. Don't you find that really and truly amazing?"

"Woof…"

Sighing deeply, he pulled his hand away from the console lid and slammed it shut. "All right, then. The gun stays here. Is that all right with you?"

"Woof…"

He sighed tiredly as he pushed open the door once again. "I guess it wouldn't hurt to talk to that moron and tell him I'm not gonna splatter his brains all over his apartment walls."

"Woof…"

"You coming? Or should I—"

140

The dog jumped out onto the pavement and stood close to him, looking up at him as he closed the door.

"I guess it's the two of us, then. Maybe he won't be so suspicious if I bring you along."

"Woof!"

Chapter 28

The doorbell, normally soft and mellow, exploded like a gunshot.

Brent Hargrove nearly dropped the cell phone. Gripping it clumsily, he pulled it away from his ear, stared at it, then turned and gawked at the apartment door. His thoughts raced, and for the longest time he wondered why he was holding the phone. Had he called someone? Had someone called him? There must be some reason why he had the damned thing in his hand.

Then he remembered.

Blocker. Samuels' thug friend had just called to tell him something weird had happened with Roth. Brent struggled to remember their conversation, but all he could gather was that Blocker hadn't done what he'd promised and, for some odd reason, couldn't remember any of the details.

Brent stared stupidly at the display. *Call ended.* That's all it said. Nothing about what had been said—or anything else. He brought the phone up to his face and looked at it. He tilted his head and kept the phone nearly a foot away from his face. "H-Hello?"

Nothing.

He tried again. "Anyone there?"

Then, just as he was about to press redial, the doorbell buzzed again. For the second time in less than a minute, Brent's pulse hammered.

Dropping the phone on the cushion beside him, he slowly straightened, then shuffled heavily across the living room floor, to the front door. For the next couple of minutes, he stood statue-like, wondering who was standing out in the hall and why he suddenly feared that his world would end horribly if he opened the door.

After his mind finally returned to its former state of relative normalcy, he realized what had transpired, then guessed who was out there in the hall.

Roth.

As Blocker had told him, Roth was parked out there in the street, no more than a hundred yards from the complex. And since Blocker had failed to scare the man off, Roth no doubt decided that Brent had sent him and decided to pay him a personal visit.

For what? Revenge? Comeuppance? Torture? Karma?

What did Roth expect to gain from facing the man who had put his wife in the hospital?

Why else would Roth want to pay him a visit? To discuss the Stock Market? Engage in some good-natured dude-bonding? Ask for sound investment advice?

What good, if anything, could come from this encounter?

The doorbell buzzed again, sending shivers down his spine. He knew right then that Roth wasn't going away. He also knew that he was going to have to handle this by himself. And that whatever he did had to be permanent—and done very soon.

Although his mind began spinning again, a few of his thoughts were clear. The one that stood out above the rest was the vivid image of the automatic pistol his brother Niles had given him for his birthday two years earlier. "For protection," Niles had said. "And it's really cool beans to drive to the gun range and see what you can do with a couple of boxes of firepower. It gives you confidence, makes you realize that if you need to defend yourself, you actually can do it."

After more than an hour of putting some impressively small groupings into his targets, Brent realized Niles was right. And that Brent was surprisingly damned good with his new pistol. And could defend himself if the situation warranted it.

Permanent, he reminded himself.

This situation definitely warrants it.

It's time for me to defend myself.

And while all the other random thoughts continued spinning wildly in his head, Brent rushed down the hall to his bedroom, where the Sig Sauer P365 sat quietly in the nightstand drawer beside his bed.

Chapter 29

Out in the hall, Owen squinted closely at the peephole.

He saw nothing. No shadows, no movement. "Maybe he's not home," he said, mostly to himself.

The dog stood three feet behind him, watching him. She made no response.

"He might have left while we were busy scaring off that big lug outside the car, and we didn't see—"

The dog made a tiny whining noise.

He turned. She'd approached the door, stopped about a foot away, and kept her left ear closest to the door.

"You think he's in there?"

The dog stared up at him and tilted her head.

"Do you sense something?"

The dog's nub shook furiously.

"Really?"

The nub continued to shake.

"Are you trying to tell me you hear something in there?" he whispered.

A tiny whine.

He continued staring at her. He didn't want to believe her but suspected that he should. He thought about all the crazy things that had been happening since last night and realized that some sort of strangeness had been guiding him ever since this dog had entered his life. This alone convinced him that he should take her instincts more seriously.

In other words, listen to this dog. She hasn't steered you wrong yet.

But he had come this far and knew that he had to face Hargrove and tell him exactly what he had done to Morgan. Maybe that was all he had to do. Maybe Hargrove had no idea how badly he had injured Morgan.

Maybe Hargrove wasn't the bastard Owen thought he was. He obviously had a few too many and lost control of his car. Frightening things happened to people all the time. Owen had driven drunk many times in the past. Like most teens whose thoughts never approached the issue of death or serious injury, he'd driven drunk after college smokers and had even made it home in one piece after nearly a dozen mixed drinks celebrating a vital football game win in senior high. After college, he had operated a vehicle while intoxicated dozens of times. Luckily, he hadn't injured himself or anyone else. But unlike most others unable to interpret the writing on the wall, he had mended his ways.

He finally realized that, even though Morgan had been the unfortunate victim in this horror, he couldn't in good conscience throw stones at the man who most likely hadn't meant something like this to happen.

And in this case, he realized that he really needed to see this from Hargrove's point of view.

Suddenly ashamed of himself, he raised his hand to the buzzer again. *I have to let this guy know that he'd put Morgan in a coma, but I also have to know how he feels about this. I'll never forgive him for it, and I'll never forget how easily he evaded*

146

punishment. But I have to understand exactly what happened, or I'll never be at peace with myself.

He pressed the buzzer and waited.

Nothing.

He waited another minute and tried again.

After another minute, nothing.

He turned to the dog. "He isn't answering."

No response.

"What now?"

The dog's eyes seemed to darken.

"Something I need to know?"

A tiny whine. The animal glanced at the door.

"Should I stay right here and try to get him to answer the door?"

No response.

"Should we leave? I mean, just walk away?"

"Woof."

"Walk away, then? Forget about talking to the jerk?"

"Woof."

"Should we do this now? I mean, right away?"

"Woof!"

He felt his pulse hasten. "Why? What I mean is, are you sure? Absolutely? Totally?"

The dog turned and trotted over to the elevator. She raised her head and gazed at the elevator door, then turned to him and whined even more urgently. She moved closer to the elevator and began to pace from one side of it to the other. Then she stopped, turned her head, and gazed at him again.

It was obvious that she wanted him to get in the elevator.

Owen could feel something dark and sour in the air. It was obviously coming from the dog, and it was telling him something was going on inside the apartment just beyond the door. The moment he began to wonder what it was, he realized that it did not really matter.

Listen to the dog, dammit!

He crossed the corridor and pressed the down button. Seconds later, they both heard the quiet whine. After what seemed an eternity, the car finally stopped. The door opened.

He followed the dog into the car.

Chapter 30

Brent Hargrove stood in the center of the living room, his hands shaking as he aimed the gun at the center of the door.

His heart raced. He shivered—not from the a/c, but from fear. Could he do this? Could he actually pull the trigger and pump a few rounds into his front door?

How would he explain his actions? What would he tell his neighbors? His landlord? The cops? The Home Association? What could he possibly tell Garrity and Richman that wouldn't immediately earn him his walking papers, or a trip to the psych ward? *Look, guys, this dude's after me because I put his wife in the hospital when I t-boned her Honda three months ago. He's been stalking me ever since, driving me up the fucking wall. I thought he was outside my door, and since I feared for my life, I decided to get my gun and pop a round or two in my door. You know, to scare him off and let him know in no uncertain terms that he was messing with the wrong—*

Ridiculous. It would make him sound mental. The Home Association would vote to have him evicted. He would face all sorts of other charges, which would amount to stiff fines and all sorts of penalties. And to make matters even worse, CF would fire him, no questions asked.

And if he managed to kill Roth, the humiliation of being evicted would no longer be an issue. Neither would being fired or facing fines and penalties. He would also be facing a murder rap, and his life would be over.

And what if no one was out there? Sure, the doorbell had buzzed. It had buzzed three separate times, and in a span of just a few minutes. Unless he was greatly mistaken, Roth was standing out there, waiting to be invited in. And he most likely wouldn't go away until the door opened.

But why?

The answer was quite simple. The man's wife was lying in a hospital bed. End of story.

Yes. It could be attributed only to that. Because he had been too damned drunk and too damned stubborn to take a cab home, Roth's wife was lying in a hospital bed. And her husband had been stalking him ever since.

Although Brent had never been married, he had been engaged a few times and knew what it was like to care about a woman. To cherish her. To want to protect her. To think of her upon rising in the morning and retiring at night, and to spend every single day with her image stamped permanently upon the inside of his eyelids. To love a babe, both physically and spiritually. To get through each day thinking of her and doing things with her. To realize that, without her, he would be nothing.

And now I'm standing here, aiming a gun at the door, ready to blow the man's head off.

Was this how he imagined his future? How his life would end?

Was this how he had always figured his existence would play out?

Here he was, gawking at his apartment door like a crazy man, a loaded pistol in his trembling hands, the barrel pointed at the peephole.

And then he realized what exactly was happening.

Or, more appropriately, *wasn't* happening.

The doorbell hadn't buzzed in several minutes.

This was when he noticed the heavy silence, which clung to him like a cold, suffocating blanket.

What was going on? Did Roth leave? Or was he still standing out there, ready to pounce the moment the door cracked open?

I really need to find out...

His pulse finally settling, Brent took a breath and lowered his cramped arms. And listened.

Silence.

He waited a little longer, alternating his gaze from the door to the wall clock fifteen feet to his left.

Still nothing.

Taking another breath, he moved his stiff legs awkwardly in the direction of the front entrance. Keeping to the right of the door, he crept closer, until his right shoulder pressed firmly against the cool plaster wall. His pulse hastened again as he very slowly and carefully inched his right ear to the wall.

He heard nothing.

He waited another minute, then moved closer to the door. Holding his breath and keeping his gun held reasonably steady, he shifted to his left, then cautiously eased his face closer to the peephole, until his left eye focused on the tiny concave opening.

A beautiful red-haired young woman stood just inches from the peephole, looking directly at him.

Chapter 31

As the elevator made its slow descent, Owen stared at the dog.

Had she been right about them leaving?

Had she smelled something coming from inside the apartment?

What was it? Death? Danger?

Would he ever know if he had done the right thing?

Even if the dog was right about all this, should he have just automatically retreated to the elevator?

While part of him thought no, the other part—the fragment that, despite the circumstances, clung stubbornly to cold logic—told him that he *had* done the right thing. And if he had, this dog had quite possibly saved his life.

Now what?

Although his first instinct was to reject his scrapping such an important decision, he realized that there was no reason whatsoever to waste negative energies on what he had just done. Why even question something like this when this dog might have been instrumental in saving his life? Why waste negative emotions on something that could have severely diminished his longevity?

Was it because his longevity didn't really mean much to him anymore? Because of Morgan's present state, he no longer cared if he lived or died?

Wasn't this why he didn't seem to care much about fate or its consequences while he'd stood out there on the walk the night before, aiming a gun at

Hargrove while heavy traffic passed just yards away? Or that he was only a second or two away from pulling that trigger when this dog had interrupted him?

He told himself that, while the dog might have actually helped him in the long run, his problem remained. Hargrove had gotten away with it again. And although Owen might have just escaped death or serious injury, he was not at all pleased with the result.

But what could he do? Just minutes ago, he'd decided—with the help of strange vibes coming from the dog, of course—to scrap his initial plan of killing Hargrove and have a direct encounter with the man. But now, after sensing that he had somehow escaped potential danger, he found that his plan was quickly returning. He now discovered that the urge to run back to the car, grab the gun, march back to Hargrove's apartment, break in and empty the load in the bastard's head, had returned with a vengeance.

Is this what he wanted?

Is this what he thought would settle the score?

Or were his emotions still running hot and wild? After all, he was just feet away from the man who had destroyed his life with Morgan, but had immediately called off his plan of revenge because of the strange actions of a dog he hadn't even known existed not twenty-four hours earlier.

The animal reached the Challenger and stared at it while waiting patiently for him to unlock the door. He slid in after her, but the moment he pulled the door shut, he noticed a shadow on his left.

A woman looking very much like Morgan was standing less than two feet from his door. She wore maroon shorts and a gold tank top—the same outfit Morgan had worn when they first met at the company picnic.

She was smiling at him.

The dog whined softly from the passenger seat.

Startled by the sound, he turned sharply and swallowed a lump in his throat as he gawked at the dog. Then he turned back toward the door. "Morgan? Is that *you*, Baby?"

The dog whined again, this time more urgently.

He turned back to the animal. His heart was thrashing and he felt light-headed. "Morgan. My wife. She's...she's *out* there. *Out there*...in the *street*!"

The dog stared blankly at him.

Confusion and frustration overtook him. Gasping, he turned around quickly.

Morgan had vanished.

Chapter 32

"Do you think that was wise? Appearing to him after what just happened?"

Her shimmering form dimming slightly, Morgan turned at the sound of her friend's voice.

Her thick red hair flowing behind her, Ava crossed the busy street just as a parade of vehicles passed quickly through her translucent form.

Morgan shrugged, then turned back to the Challenger for another glimpse of Owen. Right now, her husband was gawking frantically out the side window. He was looking both confused and panic-stricken, and she immediately felt very badly for putting him through this.

"Better not keep doing that," Ava said. "It wouldn't be particularly good for him if he saw you again, would it? It really won't help the situation, if you know what I mean. You don't want to give him a heart attack, do ya?"

Frowning, Morgan pulled her focus away from the man she loved so much and moved away from the Challenger, her form dissolving with each step, until she was no longer visible.

Ava was right. Unless...maybe she was wrong about the whole thing. Maybe Owen *hadn't* seen her at all. It had only been a brief instant, hadn't it? In the blinking of an eye? And with the heavy traffic, he might have been distracted.

But she knew she was deluding herself. Owen *had* seen her. It was obvious by his reaction. Owen wasn't the type who panicked very easily. If he *hadn't* seen her, why had he reacted like that?

Still, there was that slight chance that something else might have happened…

"Maybe he didn't actually see me," she told Ava. "I mean, in *this* traffic? And especially after what he's been going through? He seemed jittery, on edge. For all we know, he might have glimpsed something that happened across the street."

Ava stopped just a foot or two away from her and stood in the middle of the road, directly in the path of a large SUV that roared through her as it approached the turnoff at the end of the street. "Count on it," she told Morgan. "I could see your aura while you were approaching the car, and I was crossing Colonial at the time. You were glowing white, with red and gold flecks. In this world, you were as strong as you could possibly be in that instant. If he didn't see you right then, he's blind."

"Even if he isn't a true believer?"

"Are you saying he's not?"

Morgan sighed. Ava was right on—which made things more complicated at this precise moment. "Owen's a special guy. He's very perceptive, among other things. He's never been religious, but he feels and senses things most others would never admit to. And he's really a good person."

"In other words, you're saying he probably *did* see you…"

Morgan nodded.

"Don't beat yourself up," Ava said. "If I were in your shoes…"

157

Morgan suddenly felt guilty. She hadn't signed up for this. She was just heading home from the grocery that night—as she'd done dozens of times before—when the bright lights slammed into her side, turning everything dark and blurry and warm. It wasn't her fault that an idiot who had been drinking had entered her personal sphere at the wrong time. "I didn't mean to do this. I just…well, I just…you know—"

"Yeah. I know. As I just said, if I were in your shoes…"

Morgan turned back for one last peek.

"Make it quick," Ava warned. "We can't stay here. Especially since that Hargrove guy caught a glimpse of me through his peephole."

Morgan's jaw dropped. "He…he *saw* you?"

"He sure did."

"How?"

Ava shrugged. "I let him."

"But why?"

"I guess I'm just as guilty as you are. But in my case, I let my anger show off my true colors. I figured he needed some sort of comeuppance right then. After all, he *was* aiming a gun at the door, and your man was standing out in the hall, directly in the line of fire. Do the math."

Morgan shivered. "You mean…you mean he might have actually—"

"Who knows? At least I had time to warn Bella, and she managed to coax your hubby back into the elevator."

Morgan smiled. "She really *is* a special lady, isn't she?"

158

"Why do you think I sent her to him?"

"To keep Owen from doing something stupid."

"Which he very nearly did. More than once."

Morgan nodded. "I know. He's beside himself and has been that way ever since I slipped into my coma. He's a terrific guy, but very protective, and can be frightening if his buttons have been pushed. I told you he might try to turn the tables."

"That would explain his actions lately."

"Well, he loves me. After all, we had a great relationship."

Ava nodded. "But he did push the envelope, didn't he? He almost committed murder."

"But he didn't, did he?"

"Not yet…"

Morgan gasped. "You honestly think he might try *again*?"

"Don't you?"

Morgan struggled to think of some way to tell Ava she was wrong. But she couldn't. Not from what she'd seen during the last twenty-four hours. And she had to admit that Owen's temper had gotten the best of him many times in the past.

"You do, don't you?" Ava asked.

After a pause, she nodded.

"Which is why I sent Bella to protect him."

"And I appreciate it. I really and truly do."

"Good. Now that we're both on the same page again, I think we really need to get away from here. The longer we're standing so close to his car—"

"I know, I know." She sighed. "I just wanna have one last glance before—"

159

"All right. Take your one last glance. But try to keep your colors from showing. Then we've got to get out of here. It's too noisy. I can't concentrate. We still have some work to do."

Morgan turned back to Owen and blew him a kiss. "I'll see you soon, my love," she whispered. "I promise." Then she turned away and headed toward Ava, who had already started walking in the other direction. Once Morgan drew closer, the two figures meshed into one before vanishing completely.

Chapter 33

Unnerved after yanking the door open and not seeing anyone there, Brent Hargrove decided he needed a strong drink.

His legs were unsteady as he went down the hall. He managed to get through the kitchen doorway without incident but immediately realized that he had forgotten why he had come into the room. He stood there a few moments, trying to forget what he had seen in the peephole while struggling to focus on the present. Then it dawned on him.

A drink. He needed something to steady his nerves, which had come unraveled. He raised his arm to open the cabinet door but discovered that he still gripped the Sig Sauer. Cursing himself, he set the pistol on the counter and tried again. This time, he was able to do the job. He grabbed the Absolut bottle, carefully poured two inches into a clean glass, and drank it right down. Once the fiery liquid had warmed his insides, he leaned against the counter, closed his eyes, and tried to make sense of what had just happened.

Roth had come to the door.

Why the hell had he done that? The answer was simple. He wanted to come in, of course.

He splashed another inch or so of vodka into the glass and gulped it down. When the liquid warmed him up even more, he experienced some relief and discovered that his brain was functioning much more efficiently and that his thoughts were coming in more clearly.

He put the glass on the counter and rubbed his eyes.

How much more of this could he take? Sure, he'd fucked up and sent a woman to the hospital. But he was *drunk*, dammit. He hadn't meant *any* of this to happen.

But it *had* happened, and now he had to face the cold reality of what was going to happen from now on. The husband of this woman was coming after him. For revenge? Most likely. For some sort of closure? That was also a definite possibility. There was also the strong possibility that he wanted more money than what CF had given him and his wife for their troubles.

That might have been it all along. People were crazy nowadays, and greedier than ever before. The mid six figures the company had awarded the Roth's for their suffering might not have been anywhere near what the husband had wanted.

However, the amount of money might not have been the major issue after all. Brent had no idea whatsoever what the other man had in mind and needed to find some way of handling this.

But how?

And just what did all this have to do with the redheaded babe he'd seen in the peephole just moments after he'd nearly emptied the Sig into the door?

Who the hell was she?

Why was she standing at the door, staring back at him?

And most importantly, why wasn't she there when he pulled open the door?

Chapter 34

Owen tried convincing himself he had seen nothing. As he gazed out the side window, he came to the startling realization that what he glimpsed just a few minutes ago was probably just his imagination.

The image that had appeared to him was Morgan. He was certain of it. Morgan was standing there one moment but disappeared in the blinking of an eye.

What was happening to him?

Why had things turned so strange since his last visit to the hospital?

Did this all start when the dog had entered his life?

Once again he struggled to analyze why he had come back to this very same spot moments before Hargrove was involved in a traffic accident.

Then he thought about the thug who had approached his car. What was *that* all about? And why had the punk been scared off so easily?

The dog whined softly, bringing him back to reality.

It was only then that he realized he'd been staring into space, looking out but not actually seeing the passing traffic, the two teens running across the street, or the elderly lady struggling to get out of her van that was parked in the side lot of the Parkway Towers. All he saw was Morgan lying in her hospital bed, still and lifeless...and how she looked the last time she smiled at him during their last meal together, at the steak & lobster place on Colonial, less than two blocks from where Hargrove had t-boned her Honda later that same day.

Just then, the dog's paw touched his forearm, and he jumped.

Startled by his reaction, the animal pulled away.

"It's all right." He lowered his head and rubbed his eyes.

No. It was *not* all right. Nothing had been all right for the last three months, and nothing would ever be all right ever again.

But he knew he shouldn't take out his torment on this very special dog. She had been helping him through this. For all he knew, she might have even saved his life outside Hargrove's apartment.

He took a breath and tried to mellow. Once his heartrate returned to normal, he turned back to the dog. "I was just...I was out of it, if you know what I mean."

The dog's nub swished against the seat.

Yes. Of course, she knew. She was just a dog, but she knew. Even though this animal had only been with him for a day, she seemed to know his mood swings, his silences, his anger. And for some reason he could not yet comprehend, she also seemed to fully understand what he was thinking.

"I'm not sure what I saw." He was speaking out loud, but even so, he was speaking the truth.

Or *was* he? He knew what he saw. It was Morgan, although he knew there was no logical reason why her image should have appeared to him.

She had appeared nonetheless, but he just didn't know why. Or how...

And this was what made things so confusing.

The dog tilted her head.

Had he just said something? He had no idea. He didn't remember saying anything. He was so shocked about glimpsing Morgan's image that life as he knew it had just *stopped*. And because of it, nothing else registered.

The dog sat watching him. She seemed to be waiting for some sort of explanation.

"What I thought I saw," he finally said, "made no sense, and when I realized the woman I thought I saw wasn't there anymore, I kind of zoned out."

The dog cocked her left ear.

"I really don't know what happened, and I'm not sure I even *want* to know."

The dog continued watching him.

Was all this confusion the direct result of the vision?

Had this hallucination convinced him that all this was some surrealistic episode? The whole thing—the dog's sudden appearance, Hargrove's traffic accident, the weirdness at the penthouse, and the vision of Morgan—reeked of weirdness. Creepiness. Irrationality. The supernatural. Magic.

He wanted to ask the dog to give him a sign that would tell him if she knew why she had first approached him—if she could remember anything before the moment she walked up to him.

If she could tell him anything *at all*.

But just before he could say anything, she stared at him and the image of his apartment flickered brightly in his head.

"My place?" he asked her.

A soft whine.

"We need to go back to my place?"

The dog blinked.

"You mean now?"

Her nub swished eagerly.

"You're saying we should go back there right this second?"

Another whine.

He sighed. "I guess we're going back home, then."

"Woof!"

Chapter 35

Brent Hargrove poured more vodka into his glass and sucked it right down.

He put the glass on the counter and told himself he was going crazy and needed to do something about it. Something drastic. Something that would stop all this insanity. And since that idiot friend of Randy Samuels had fucked up the works, some other solution would have to be arranged.

Stan D'Angelo, one of the major board members of CF, had deep connections with the investment community as well as in other fields, which included various enterprises in New York City, where he originally came from. Rumors of former ties to organized crime seemed far-fetched but had never been questioned or investigated. Brent had heard from several different sources that D'Angelo knew many powerful and influential people, both in business and in other ventures. These people were known for their connections all over the world, many of them with the ability to make and break careers, as well as eliminating nuisances regarding both personal and business dealings. He had also heard several stories supporting the fact that D'Angelo prided himself in doing favors for people he considered his friends.

Brent had helped the man a couple of years ago by finding a suitable banquet room on the spur of the moment for one of D'Angelo's get-togethers with his New York connections, many of whom had invested heavily in CF interests. D'Angelo was extremely grateful for Brent's last-minute miracle and had told him that whenever he needed a favor, all he had to do was ask.

Grinning in relief, Brent grabbed the cell phone on the kitchen counter. *Roth,* he thought wildly as the vicious scenario developed in his head, *you're about to have your lights put out.*

His alcohol-blurred vision gradually returned the moment he opened his personal address book to look up D'Angelo's number.

Chapter 36

While driving back to Winter Park, Owen could not stop thinking about the vision he had seen. He just could not convince himself that it was a figment of his imagination. And the fact that Morgan disappeared the moment he turned away merely substantiated this phenomenon.

It was all in your head, he kept telling himself. *It must be that because Morgan is all you've been thinking about for the last three months.*

He parked in his spot and got out of the Challenger. The dog jumped out and trotted over to the bushes beneath his living room window. He waited until she had finished before walking up the front stoop and unlocking the door.

Once the dog hurried inside, he followed, then closed the door. She led the way into the kitchen and went right over to her water dish. He approached the sink, filled a large glass with fresh water, then waited until she moved away. He filled up her dish, grabbed the bourbon bottle from the cabinet and poured two inches into his glass. Sighing wearily, he drank it down in one swallow. It burned, relaxing him. He leaned against the counter and thought about the last half hour. The dog was sitting just a few feet away, watching him. He raised his empty glass. "This is what civilized people do when we want to forget all about what's going on in our head that really shouldn't be there in the first place."

The dog swished her nub.

"I know, I know. Stupid, right? Especially since this sucker seems to be empty."

No response.

Owen poured more bourbon into his glass and sat down on one of the stools. He had another sip, put the glass down, and stared at it. The dog whined. He glanced at the food dish. "Hungry?"

No response.

He got up, grabbed the bag of dry food he had bought earlier, scooped out half a cup, and dumped it in her bowl. The dog watched him but made no move to go to it.

"It's there when you want it." He sat back down, had another sip of bourbon, and began staring at the dog once again. "I saw Morgan. At least I thought I did. It might have been an illusion, and probably was...but it sure as hell looked like her."

The dog swished her nub.

"I saw her out there on Broadway. After we got back in the car. I was sitting right beside you, and when I turned, there she was, standing outside the car. She wasn't in the hospital at all, she was right there, beside the car. And she was dressed in the same outfit she wore when we first met."

Silence.

He watched the animal's eyes for a few moments. He quickly found that he didn't like what he saw in them. "Something tells me you already knew all that."

No reaction.

He had no idea what else to say. The dog couldn't help him with this, could she? What he had

171

seen was an illusion. In the real world, Morgan was lying comatose in a hospital bed. There was no way she could appear to him outside his car on Broadway Avenue…

Was there?

Yep, his imagination. That is what it boiled down to. A hallucination. Hope. Blind faith. For all he knew, he could be losing his sanity. What was next? Her voice in his ear, telling him weird things?

He had another sip of the bourbon. The dog continued staring at him.

"Worried your new owner might be losing his nut?"

A soft whine.

"If I were you, I would, too."

The animal cocked her left ear.

"Any suggestions?"

Silence.

He shrugged. "Tell me…how the hell am I supposed to act? She's the love of my life. She's been lying in a coma for months. There hasn't been noticeable brain activity for weeks. And to make things even worse, no one thinks she's ever coming out of it."

The dog whined softly again.

He blinked. "What's *that* supposed to mean?"

Another whine.

"Are you trying to tell me something?"

The nub swished eagerly.

"Do you know something I don't?"

Another whine.

Suddenly curious, he stared at the dog, hoping he could read something in her big brown eyes. At

172

first, he saw nothing. But then he thought he saw some sort of sparkle that might actually mean something.

"Do you know she's in a coma?"

A soft whine.

"Does that mean yes?"

The dog blinked.

"Does that blink mean yes?"

The nub swished.

He raised his glass with a shaky hand and finished his drink. Then he put the glass down. "Tell me something. Is Morgan *ever* gonna come out of it?"

No response.

"Do you know? Do you have *any* idea? Can you give me any sign whatsoever? Or am I just being a shithead?"

A soft whine.

"I know. I'm being a shithead, right?"

Silence.

"They've asked me three times if I wanted to turn off the machine. The last time was yesterday."

The nub swished.

He shook his head as the memories flooded back. "I didn't say a damned word. I just turned around and walked away."

A soft whine.

He shrugged. "If I had said *anything*, I knew it would haunt me for the rest of my life."

Another whine.

"I know, I know. I'm a coward. But I'm desperate, dammit. Look at me. Here I am, talking to a *dog* about medical advice."

173

"Woof…"

Owen nodded. "I'm stupid. Yeah, I know it. But can you blame me? I've got nothing left. Nothing. Nada. El zilcho."

The dog looked sad.

"I know what you're thinking. And no, I'm not about to do anything stupid, okay? I'm just thinking out loud."

No response.

"If you've got anything you'd like me to know right now, I wouldn't mind you giving me a hint. Believe me, anything will do."

Silence.

Briefly he considered going back to the Parkway Towers again. Then he thought of how he felt and reminded himself how stupid he could be at times.

"I'd drive back to Hargrove's apartment, but I've had entirely too many of these." He held up his empty glass. "I quit driving drunk years ago when I finally began developing some serious brain cells. Not like him. Not like Hargrove. He'd think nothing of doing something as stupid as that. Look what he's already done."

A soft whine.

"You wouldn't want me to drive in this condition, would you?"

The dog tilted her head.

"I'd call him—just to let him know I'm not coming after him. Would that be all right with you?"

Another whine.

"I'd still like to blow his head off, you know. But that wouldn't be very smart, would it?"

The nub swished.

Owen stared at the animal for quite a while before he spoke again. "The funny thing is, ever since you showed up, I really don't *want* to cap him anymore."

The dog's left ear twitched.

"Can you tell me why?"

Silence.

"Could you tell me why I saw Morgan's image outside the car?"

A whine.

"Can't you go into just a little more detail? I know you had something to do with that. I just don't know how."

Another whine.

"Don't want to say anything?"

Silence.

Owen got up from the stool. The moment he stood, he realized just how much bourbon he had put away. A little woozy, he staggered down the hall, dropped into the living room couch and stretched out.

The dog followed him in. She sat on her haunches in front of the couch, watching him.

"Mind if I sleep this one off? I don't know if you're fully aware of this, but I've had a pretty damned rough day."

"Woof."

He thought about what he should do the next day. Another trip to the Parkway Towers? Or should he just say hell with the formalities and deck the son

175

of a bitch the moment the door opened? A coldcocking would be severe but was considerably less brutal than five full metal jackets applied to the face. Besides, it might make him feel better, and he wouldn't have to worry about spending the rest of his life in prison for murder.

"We'll just see how I feel when I get up," he told the dog, who watched as he adjusted the pillow under his head.

"Sorry about the couch being so small. We didn't have a dog when we bought it. Otherwise, it would be much bigger." He sighed and forced himself not to glance at the picture of Morgan that sat on the shelf facing the couch. Beautiful, smiling Morgan dressed in a maroon bikini during their honeymoon at Miami Beach. "Maybe I'll buy a bigger one later on, if I can get through all this shit without killing myself or turning into a hopeless lunatic."

A barely audible whine.

"I promise it'll be big enough for both of us to lie on at the same time. How does that sound?"

The dog watched as he settled into a more comfortable position. Owen closed his eyes and began thinking about the next day, but the bourbon quickly made everything dark, and in just moments he felt himself drifting toward the soft blackness of sleep.

Chapter 37

"Course I remember ya."

Stan D'Angelo's voice sounded as loud and as powerful as ever. "You're the guy arranged that shindig for me on the fly when everyone else seemed more worried about what would happen if they didn't make me smile."

"That sounds about right." Brent Hargrove laughed. "When people find out that a guy has friends in the Mob—"

D'Angelo snorted. "They think severed horse heads and dead fish and all that other good shit that makes for terrific scary stuff in movies. I guess ya know I really don't go in for that shtick, right?"

Brent winced at the sudden disappointment but knew better than voice it. "Right."

"But I still do right by my friends. I been this way since I grew up in Brooklyn. If ya don't do right by your buds, then what the hell good are ya? And since ya did me a favor, I consider you a friend—right?"

"I hope so…"

"Good. So I guess ya called because you'd like me to do something for ya…"

"Well…"

"Don't ass around, *paisano*. Just tell me what ya need…"

He told D'Angelo about Roth stalking him but left out the major tidbit about his sending Roth's wife to the hospital. He didn't feel the need to tell the man everything. He thought that by giving him the whole story, D'Angelo might balk at helping him. It was widely observed that D'Angelo treated women with respect and admiration. The man might not appreciate doing a favor for someone who had put a girl in the hospital. Besides, he wasn't sure how deep D'Angelo's Italian roots were; he just figured that he shouldn't tempt fate by telling him anything that might sour this. Bad enough Samuels' thug buddy had bailed on him.

"So…what're ya asking me to do? Ya want this guy gone? Like maybe permanent? If that's the case, I really ain't your guy, *paisano*. I don't go in for that crap and don't wanna waste any sleep over it. I spent a little time behind bars when I was a kid—petty shit and all that other stupid crap every *stronzo* does when he's seventeen and feeling his oats. But I'm all grown up now and don't wanna do anything that'll put me on the wrong side of the law. You meet all kinds of shit in the gen pop, and you find out that no matter how tough ya thought you were, you ain't no match for some of these stiffs walking around, looking for a new bitch to wrap their paws around. I turned the big five-oh last year and believe me, it ain't no picnic. Besides, I know how the law treats—"

"I just want him scared off." Brent was tired of listening to the man's inhibitions and just wanted to get on with this.

A pause. "*Just* scared off?"

"Yeah."

"So then, ya want somebody to—"

"I don't know what I want. Not really. I just don't want him bothering me anymore. If you'd just consider—"

The doorbell buzzed.

Brent froze. His pulse hastened.

"*Paisano?*"

Brent could not move. He stared at the door, wondering who was standing out there in the hall and knowing he didn't have the courage to get up and walk over to the peephole.

Was Roth out there?

It had to be Roth, didn't it? At this time of day? Who else *could* it be?

But what if it wasn't? What if it was someone else?

His heart pounding, Brent Hargrove gawked at the door. Should he or shouldn't he answer it? What if it *was* Roth? What if Roth had come back again, this time to settle the score? What if he broke down the door this time? What if—

"*Paisano...*"

The sudden abrupt voice made him jump.

It was D'Angelo again. The man he had just called. The man whose help he wanted. The man who might actually be able to get Roth off his back.

The man who might bring normalcy back into his life.

The doorbell buzzed again, and he practically jumped out of his skin.

This was insane—something he just could not handle. What the hell was he supposed to do? Answer it? Just sit here and wait? For what? For the buzzing to stop? And then what? Stay locked up in this apartment forever?

What about his job? His career?

He couldn't just shitcan everything in his life because he was suddenly afraid to answer the damned door!

Well? *Could* he?

"*Paisano*? You there?"

What was happening? What was going on?

Why did he suddenly want to be a thousand miles from here?

Why had everything become so frightening? So dark? So evil?

So terrifyingly hopeless?

Just then, his phone beeped, indicating another call coming in. He glanced at the display but couldn't make out what it said. His vision had blurred, but he rubbed his eyes with his free hand, then carefully squinted at the display. Then, after several long, agonizing seconds, he could make it out.

LANA D.

It took him forever to recall the name. Then it registered.

Lana? What the fuck?

He gazed at the display, squinting at the message. It said:

forgot necklace

The back of his neck bristled. An image of the heavy black mane immediately returned, and with it, a wave of hot rage and confusion.

180

Who the fuck did this bitch think she was? His world was coming apart and all she cared about were her fucking earrings! Damn her all to hell! The stupid bitch—hadn't she done enough to him outside the Mall, when he'd nearly smeared that big-mouthed twerp all over the pavement?

I don't need this! Not now! And surely not from her!

Everything was coming apart at the seams. His world was turning into total oblivion, and now he was getting a call from a nasty, selfish bitch who had cursed him, turned her back on him, and marched out of his life.

And all this because of the bastard Roth!

I can't do this. I can't...I can't...this is too much...this is—

Think, man...think!

The gun. It lay on its side on the cushion beside him, just two feet away. All he had to do was—

The doorbell again.

I can't do this! I can't! I really and truly can't!

"*Paisano?*" It was that same abrupt voice in his ear. That same damned voice. "What the hell is going on?"

This was too much. Entirely too much!

He dropped the phone and picked up the gun. His body shook as he got up from the couch and shuffled over to the door. He stopped just five feet away, where the carpeting ended and became the large stone tiles forming the entrance.

One more time. If that damned doorbell buzzed one more time, he was going to—

Buzz!

His heart rate instantly turned chaotic as a deafening explosion ricocheted in his ears.

A giant lump forming in his throat, Brent Hargrove raised the gun. Gripping it with both hands, he held his breath as he began to pull the trigger, again and again and again…

Until all eight bullets had penetrated the center of the door.

Chapter 38

Her translucent form dim, Morgan Roth stood outside the Parkway Towers apartment building on Colonial Drive, watching the commotion outside the ornate front entrance.

Lights flashing, an ambulance stopped abruptly in the middle of the street. Dressed in paramedic uniforms, a tall blond-haired guy and a slender dark-haired girl jumped out, rushed to the back, and yanked open the doors. They hauled out a gurney and rapidly pushed it down the walk leading to the double glass doors of the building.

Two OPD uniforms gathered near the curb, keeping gawkers from getting too close. A third cop got out of his patrol car. He walked over to the other two, spoke briefly, then hurried toward the building.

Ava's fiery red mane suddenly appeared amid the growing crowd.

"What's happened?" Morgan asked. "Weren't we just back at the hospital, watching those nurses parading around my bed and checking my vitals?"

Ava nodded. "I figured we needed to be here. I was right."

"So...what happened? And where were you?" As Morgan gawked at her friend, she suddenly felt the same twinge of fear she had been worried about for some time. Ava was about to leave her, and Morgan realized yet again that she wasn't prepared to say goodbye to this beautiful lady. "I thought...that is, I figured you'd be—"

"Not yet, my friend. I still have a little time. I sensed something weird going on, so I brought us here and went in there to see if I was right."

"About what?"

"About your man not needing our help anymore."

"Really?"

Ava nodded.

Still confused, Morgan turned back to the chaos. "What's going on in there?"

"I do believe the sick soul who put you in a coma will no longer be a problem."

Morgan's eyes grew. This sounded too good to be true. "Don't tell me he's...he's not—"

"No, but he's no longer a threat. And judging by what happened in there, I'd say that he now wishes he were dead."

"What happened?"

"From what I heard, he lost his mind and shot someone through the apartment door."

"Oh my God... Really? It wasn't—who was it?"

"It was a woman, I'm afraid. A young woman with long black hair. She didn't seem to be much more than twenty-five or so. She was very pretty, and I'm reasonably sure I heard someone say her name was Lana. They were going through her handbag when I drifted over."

"And that man—that Hargrove guy—just *shot* her?"

"Right through the door, they said."

"Why would he *do* such a thing? That poor young woman. Did that man even know her?"

184

"Not sure. Like I said, I just got there right after it happened. It was a shame, wasn't it? But it could have been much worse."

"How do you mean?"

"Let me put it this way. We're both extremely glad that someone else wasn't shot."

Morgan turned toward Broadway Avenue and saw right off that Owen's Challenger was no longer parked along the curb. Then she smiled when she remembered that Bella had coaxed Owen to drive back to their apartment.

Just then, Ava looked sad.

"Ava? What's wrong?"

She smiled weakly. "I'm afraid…I guess it's time. For me. Right now, in fact."

"Really?" Morgan felt something tug sharply in her chest.

"I'm afraid so…"

"Is there any way to delay—"

"It is my time to leave. I must help someone else now."

Morgan shivered as the sadness quickly overwhelmed her. "But we didn't…I haven't had the chance to…to—"

Ava smiled again, this time with tears in her eyes. "It's not necessary, my dear friend. I am glad we had this time to ourselves, though. I'll cherish it."

"So will I."

Ava began fading.

Morgan's eyes also filled. She reached out. "When will I…when will…when will we—"

185

"One day. But right now, you really need to go back and live the rest of your life. Your man's waiting."

It only took her a moment to realize what Ava had just told her. "Then…I'm about to—"

"Yes."

"Are you sure? I mean…absolutely sure?"

"Yes, my dear friend. It wasn't your time."

Morgan sighed in relief. But just then, Ava faded a little more, and Morgan realized that the most wonderful lady she had ever known was about to vanish. "But can't we have just another moment or—"

"I'm afraid not. At least, not in this life. But I *will* look in on you from time to time, believe me."

Morgan wanted to ask about Bella. In that same moment, Ava suddenly smiled. Her form brightened, and Morgan knew right then that her friend was about to vanish.

Their hands touched. Briefly. Morgan felt the warmth of Ava's touch. A moment later, the warmth was gone.

And so was Ava.

Morgan looked up at the sky. "So long, my dear friend. I will truly miss you."

PART 3 - THE THIRD DAY

Chapter 39

Owen awoke to the sound of his cell phone buzzing from the kitchen.

Groaning, he turned over. His head throbbed, most likely from the bourbon he sucked down the night before. On a whim, he pushed himself up and, squinting, focused on the living room window, which faced east. The brightness pressing against the drapes and the blinds told him it was morning.

Morning? Seriously? He had actually slept through the night?

Strange. Since Morgan had been in the hospital, he hadn't slept more than an hour or so at a time. What was so different now? What had changed?

The cell phone buzzed again.

It was probably a telemarketer. He had been getting bombarded during the last few weeks. He was damned sure that this would be no different.

He lay back down and closed his eyes. Hell with them. Hell with everyone, as a matter of fact. It was easy to dismiss everything and everyone when your head was throbbing like a tom-tom. He reached up and gently massaged his temples. The throbbing persisted.

The cell buzzed again.

Dammit. Go away!

"Woof..."

Startled by the sound, he raised his head. The dog was sitting there, just a foot away. The expression on her face was something he had never seen before. She seemed worried. Or afraid.

"You trying to tell me something?"

"Woof..." She turned her head toward the kitchen.

The cell buzzed again.

"Woof!"

He gazed at the dog and tried even harder to read her expression. He'd never before heard her "speak" to him as urgently as she'd just done. It worried him.

"You want me to get that?"

"Woof!" Just as urgently.

Another buzz.

With a loud grunt, Owen pushed himself into a sitting position. After taking a deep breath, he forced himself to stand and nearly lost his balance. *The damned booze...* He fought the wooziness, maintaining his balance as he staggered down the hall, to the kitchen.

He stared at the cell phone before picking it up. A telemarketer? At first he suspected it was, but the dog obviously thought otherwise. The dog was trying to tell him it was important. She wanted him to answer it. And judging by what had been happening lately, he was certain that he should see what this was all about.

He glanced at the display. *Orlando Regional.* The hair on the back of his neck bristled. The hospital. This meant Morgan. Which also meant important.

Please don't let this be the end, he thought, trembling. *Please don't...*

188

His finger twitched as it carefully moved over the *TALK* option. "Y-Yes?" He barely heard his own voice.

"Mr. Roth?" asked a soft, low-pitched female voice.

He continued trembling. "Speaking..."

"Sir, this is Orlando Regional Hospital calling."

Morgan. The worst had happened. His heart hammered violently. He was afraid it would break right out of his chest. It took considerable effort to lean against the doorway to keep from collapsing.

"Y-Yes...?" He was surprised his voice still worked.

"Sir, we have good news for you this morning."

It took him several long moments to comprehend what the lady on the other end of the line had just said. *Good news for you this morning.*

Good news. For you.

Just what in heaven's name did *that* mean?

He took several breaths before he could locate his voice this time. When he felt confident enough, he whispered, "G-*Good* news?"

"Yes, sir. This concerns Mrs. Roth."

His pulse thrashed. "Y-Yes?"

"Mrs. Roth...your wife...she has come out of her coma."

His entire body instantly turned numb.

Mrs. Roth...your wife...she has come out of her coma...

A spike of ice climbed sluggishly up his spine. He thought for a moment that he was hearing things. He had heard her incorrectly. She had said something totally different.

189

Come out of her coma...

He suspected that what he'd just heard was something right out of a dream. He was still dreaming. He had the strongest urge to rush into the living room and see if he was still sleeping on the couch.

Come out of her coma!

"Mr. Roth?"

"Y-Yes?" It took three him tries to get the word out.

"Are you all right?"

"Did you...did you just say...what I *thought* you said?"

"Yes, Mr. Roth."

He had to hear it again. Once wasn't quite enough. Once just wouldn't cut it. He needed her to repeat it. To tell him again. To let him know that he wasn't hearing things. He had to know that he might not be leaving the planet and going straight to hell so quickly after all.

His pulse fluttered wildly as he said, "Humor me. *Please* repeat what you just said."

"Mr. Roth, your wife has come out of her coma."

Come out of her coma.

Morgan was no longer in her coma. She'd *come out of it*.

She was *alive* again. *Alive*.

Alive!

He struggled to find his voice this time. He had to clear his throat again, take a giant breath, then clear his throat yet again. And when he was finally able to let the words out, they came out very softly, very sluggishly, and did not sound even remotely like his normal voice. "Really? Seriously?"

"Yes, sir. She's regained consciousness and has been asking to see you."

Chapter 40

Morgan was sitting up in bed when Owen reached the doorway of her hospital room.

He froze abruptly and stood there in tense silence, not knowing what to do or say. He had never seen her look so beautiful. Her hair was unwashed and matted, some of it clinging wetly to her forehead and right cheek, yet her face glowed like that of an angel, her head propped up with pillows, her large hazel eyes glossy, pointed directly at him.

Her expression was one of confusion and fear, yet he could clearly see a shadow of the familiar smile he thought he would never glimpse again. The tiny crescent dimple that frequently appeared near the right side of her mouth was visible, telling him that she felt well enough to smile. This, more than anything else, conveyed the clear message that she had finally come back to him.

But how had this happened?

How had she magically come out of her coma when, just hours ago, everyone had obviously given up, and wanted his written permission to turn off her machine?

How had she successfully recovered from her near-fatal trauma when no visible sign of improvement had shown on her monitors since they brought her into this room?

Did it really matter? Did he care how this happened? Did he feel the need to hunt down her doctors and ask them for some sort of medical explanation to justify Morgan's sudden recovery from three solid months in a seemingly irreversible coma?

Was he stupid enough or foolish enough to agonize over the little stuff, when the most important person in his life was lying there just ten feet away, smiling at him and anxiously waiting for him to rush over and smother her with kisses and hugs?

Just then, he heard her voice. It was soft and weak, and barely audible. But he heard it, nonetheless. It was this one single phenomenon that shook him out of his clueless state.

"C'mon in…stay awhile…"

The sound of her voice fired up his spirit, rejuvenating him. He forced himself out of his statue-like trance and rushed over. It was a difficult task, but he successfully managed to wrap his arms around her and kiss her warm, moist face as carefully as he possibly could without hurting her.

Then, without warning, the tears came. They emerged thick and hot, covering his cheeks. He didn't care. The love of his life had come back, and now, for the first time in three months, his heartbeat had finally returned to normal.

"You're crying," Morgan whispered in his ear.

He couldn't reply; he just nodded.

"You're not *sad* that I'm back, are ya?"

Surprised at her question, he pulled away and gawked at her. She was still smiling weakly. He sighed in relief. Morgan was indeed back and, as always, teasing him. "Just a little," he said, forcing himself to keep his tone light. "I was just about to start scoping Orlando for a replacement." He shrugged. "But since two of my favorite strip clubs have already gone under—"

She elbowed him in the side. The blow, hardly her best effort, was much weaker than usual. "I'd cut out your heart...if you had one."

He felt himself softening again. He wasn't in the mood to joke about this. Not yet, anyway. But he knew he had to remain strong—at least, for her sake. He had to be himself—the person she knew so well and loved so deeply. The guy she could always count on. She needed him to be himself. Their joking had always been their strongest bond.

However, what she just said was something he could not make light of. Despite his efforts, his true feelings emerged before he had the chance to keep them at bay. "Doing that wouldn't be as hard as you'd think," he whispered.

"And why not?"

"My heart nearly broke three months ago."

A frown quickly replaced her smile. "I didn't expect you to give up so easily."

"I didn't. That's why I never told them to turn you off."

"Is that the *only* reason?"

"I never gave up. Not for an instant."

"I know."

"You do?"

"I know you, don't I?"

"By now, you should."

She gently touched his arm. "I knew you were much too strong—and entirely too stubborn—to let this beat you."

194

He took a breath. "I *thought* I was..."

"If you didn't let them turn me off—"

"I didn't do it just for me."

"No?"

"I knew it wouldn't have been something you'd want. You'd never give up, either."

She closed her eyes and sighed tiredly. "But I did give up."

He could tell by her tone that she truly meant what she said. "Really?"

A nod.

"Well, what happened to turn all this around?"

She went silent and began staring at the wall facing them. "I honestly don't know."

"You must have *some* idea…"

"I had this dream. I met someone. A beautiful lady who came to me and told me things."

"Really? This happened during…when you were comatose?"

Her expression was grave. "It must have."

He gazed at her in confusion. "You don't sound too certain."

"I'm not. But it's the only thing that makes sense."

"I talked to a few of the doctors not long after they brought you in. I asked them about stuff like that and they said you don't have dreams while you're comatose. Hallucinations, yes. But not—"

"Whatever it was, it happened. You don't believe me, do you?"

The nurse came in. "Sir, if you wouldn't mind, we need to do some things…"

He remained silent. He was still trying to figure out what Morgan had just told him.

"Sir?"

He pulled himself out of his puzzlement. "Sorry. Yes, I understand."

His mind was in a daze as he got up and shuffled out of the room.

Chapter 41

Ten minutes later, the nurse came out of the room and smiled at Owen. "You can go back in now."

"Thank you." He noticed Morgan's pensive expression as he approached her bed. She lay in the same position but seemed to be staring into space. He could tell something was bothering her. "What's wrong, baby?"

She sighed and closed her eyes. "I'm thinking more about my dream."

"Tell me about it."

A shrug. "The more I try to remember, the hazier it becomes."

He smiled. "Most dreams are like that, you know."

"I know, but this one should be different."

"Why?"

"I don't know. Maybe it's because I believe the woman in my dream helped pull me out of my coma, somehow."

"You have any idea how?"

"I honestly don't think I would have made it if she hadn't been there."

"Whaddya mean?"

"Parts of it seemed so *real*. That woman was actually *there*. In my dream. And she was there for *me*."

He found himself skeptical but didn't think this was the right time to argue with her. "Well, you did say she told you things. Remember that?"

Morgan nodded. "But I just can't remember what those things were."

"Well, whatever they were, they worked, because you obviously came through this all right."

"I'm almost positive that I hadn't seen her before. But I have this strong feeling that she became a friend. And that she saved me."

"Do you remember anything else? About the dream itself, I mean. Any idea where you were?"

Morgan closed her eyes. She didn't speak right off. Then, after a large sigh, she opened her eyes and looked at him. "At first, there was darkness. I was scared, of course, because I thought I had died. But it wasn't long before I realized I *hadn't* died, and that I actually felt good. I was convinced nothing would ever hurt me again, and that I was okay with whatever was happening while I was there, in the darkness."

"Tell me more about the darkness."

"Like I said, it came first. Then my vision cleared, and a strange bright haze smothered the darkness. And when this happened, I felt comfortable and warm. It was like being in a beautiful, peaceful place, and all I heard was a heavy silence. But the silence felt wonderful, and nothing hurt anymore..."

"You were in this strange place before you met this lady?"

"She was already there."

"Do you happen to remember anything specific about her? Did she tell you anything about herself?"

Once again, Morgan looked pensive. "She never did say why she was there, or even how she

198

got there. There seemed to be a golden haze around her, but I could tell she was about my age, I guess, and slender, and she had fiery red hair."

"Can you remember *anything* she told you?"

"I'm trying to, but..." She shook her head. "Everything else seems a blur."

"Everything?"

"Most of the things she told me seemed to be important, but since I can't remember any of them now..." She shrugged.

"Like I said, dreams can be very vague."

"I know, but like I said, this one is different. I mean, it didn't seem like a normal dream. Everything was clear as a bell—that is, until I woke up. I really feel that if it hadn't been for that woman, I might not have come out of my coma."

"But you did. That's the important thing."

Morgan nodded but remained silent.

Owen wondered what he could say that would ease her mind. He had no idea what had happened, nor could he think of anything he could say to her that would give her comfort. But amid his frustration, something popped up in his head and he realized he needed to understand something that had been bothering him. He didn't want to bring it up for fear of upsetting her but knew that it had become an important issue, and that it had to be addressed. "I need to talk to you about something."

She tilted her head. "What is it, baby?"

"I saw you...yesterday evening."

"What?"

"You were standing outside my car."

"Where was *this*?"

"On Broadway Avenue. Just across the street from the Parkway Towers."

She blinked. "What were you doing *there*?"

"The man who ran into you. Hargrove lives there. He's got a penthouse apartment. I was—"

"Owen…what did you do?"

"To him? Nothing."

"Then what were you—"

"I was stalking him." There was no other way of phrasing it.

She stared at him in that special way that made him feel like an idiot. She'd been doing that ever since they met, and she was good at it. But he knew that in nearly every single case, he deserved it. He also knew what was coming. "You said you didn't do anything?"

"Not a damned thing."

"But you wanted to."

"Of course I wanted to. I wanted to empty my piece into his thick skull."

"But you didn't."

"Nope."

She smiled. "I'm *so* glad…"

"I wanted to knock on his door, tell him who I was and why I was there. Then I was gonna—"

"The important thing is that you didn't. And we're together again."

"I know." He gazed into her beautiful eyes and realized once again how lucky he was.

"I want you to forget all that," she said after a pause.

"I'm trying." He knew he wouldn't but saw no point in telling her otherwise. "Let's get back to what we were talking about."

"You actually saw me outside your car?"

"I sure did."

"What was I doing?"

"Just standing there, smiling at me."

"Did anything else happen?"

He shrugged. "I kinda took my eyes off you for one moment. Then you just disappeared."

"Just like that?"

"Just like that." He didn't want to tell her about the dog until they went back to the apartment. He wanted it to be a surprise and knew she'd fall in love with the animal at first glance—just as he had done.

"All I can think of is that you might have just imagined me there."

"Well, I *was* thinking about you, so…"

Morgan touched his arm. "The mind knows how to play tricks, doesn't it?"

"It sure does."

"I just wish it would start working right so it could tell me what happened."

"All you remember is that woman with red hair? And that she told you things that brought you out of your coma?"

"Basically."

"Anything else?"

Morgan went silent again, staying this way for several minutes.

He began getting worried. "Baby? You still in there somewhere?"

201

Silence.

"Baby?"

Just then, she stiffened. Her eyes were wide when she said, "I just remembered something about her. Something she told me."

"What was it?"

"It was about herself. About something that was very dear to her."

"Go on…"

"She told me about…her dog."

***

"Her dog."

The woman Morgan had seen in her dream had a dog.

Owen's brain jumped into overload. Was it possible? Could the friend in Morgan's hallucination have been talking about—

Was this the same dog?

Impossible. His mind had gone berserk again, and his imagination had taken over.

Steady… Don't get ahead of yourself. You need to find out about this first. Otherwise, you might as well forget about everything else and just check yourself in to the nearest mental ward.

His voice was shaky as he asked her the next question. "Baby…this woman you saw…and talked to…she…had a *dog*?"

"Yes. And I believe she said her dog's name was Bella."

"Bella?"

Morgan smiled. "For some strange reason, this seems to be the only thing I can truly remember about her. That is, other than her long red hair and how beautiful she was. The other stuff she told me?" She shrugged. "As hard as I try to remember, it seems to be gone. I have this strange feeling that maybe I'm not supposed to remember anything."

Owen remained silent as the images in his brain continued jumping around like crazy fireflies.

Could it really be true? Could the dog that had come into his life two days earlier actually be the dog the redheaded woman was talking about? Was it her dog? And if it was, what was the dog doing with Owen? How did she find him in the first place?

Could any of this be happening?

"Baby, you look...well, weird." Morgan was watching him closely. "What's wrong? Does this have anything to do with—"

"Tell me more about this woman's dog." He could feel his pulse hammering, his blood rushing through his veins.

Morgan blinked. "What's going on, baby? Why are you acting as if—"

"Tell me about the dog, Morgan." He tried not to sound desperate, but it was getting more difficult.

"Why do you want to know?"

"Describe the dog."

"I never saw her."

"Your friend didn't tell you anything about her? Other than her name?"

"No. Just that she had this amazing dog, and that she had this wonderful ability to read her thoughts and—"

"Her name was Bella. A *she*. Her dog was female."

"Yes, baby...."

Owen remained silent. His thoughts were making him dizzy as the picture formed more clearly in his head.

Morgan looked worried. "Please tell me what's got you so freaked out, baby…"

"The dog. Tell me. I have to know. I have to know everything you can tell me. And I have to know *now*."

"But *why*?"

Owen didn't reply.

"Baby, you're scaring me…"

He pulled himself out of the turmoil that had taken over his mind and forced himself to focus on her. His wife. The woman he loved more than anything in the world. The woman who had finally come back to him and was now gawking at him with the most frightening expression on her face.

The woman who deserved to know everything that was going on in his head.

"Baby? *Please* talk to me…"

He took a breath and forced himself to stay calm. "Unless I'm totally wrong about all this, your friend's dog is waiting for us back at the apartment."

Chapter 42

The apartment was empty.

Owen and Morgan stood in the doorway, gazing into the living room. Owen concentrated on the sofa, expecting his vision to correct itself to the semidarkness of the room and eventually produce the form of the beautiful animal sitting there, her nub swishing as she eagerly watched his return...

But no such form appeared.

A sinking feeling filled his being, and he stood quite still, a heavy sadness overcoming him.

The trip from the hospital, though just a few miles, had been extremely unsettling. Owen's mind, beset in turmoil, refused to focus. Morgan was back. According to her doctors, her recovery had been miraculous. But it happened nonetheless, and now, after three long, stressful months, the love of his life had returned.

I truly am blessed, he told himself over and over, holding her hand while trying to concentrate on his driving. *Morgan's back. Aside from the bruising and other minor problems from her accident, she seems unchanged, and well on her way to recovery. She remembers me and doesn't seem to be suffering from any visible aspect of mental trauma. Her mind's just as sharp as ever, and her wit hasn't suffered one bit. Our life will return to the same state of bliss it was before.*

What, then, was distracting him from focusing completely on his wife's homecoming?

The answer was simple.

He could not stop thinking about the dog.

And now that they had returned home and discovered that Bella was nowhere in sight, Owen realized that his joy for having his wife return home had been greatly diminished, and he found himself at a complete loss.

"She's not here," he said, mostly to himself. He turned to Morgan and suddenly felt guilty for not taking his wife in his arms. But he couldn't help it. Incredible as it sounded, Morgan had returned, but his life suddenly felt incomplete. "She's gone. She just...disappeared."

Morgan's expression suggested that she totally understood. "A wonderful dog came into your life at a very stressful time. You were vulnerable, filled with anger and frustration and a hundred other emotions that made you susceptible to every single thing that came your way. Can't you just accept that?"

"I wish I could."

"This isn't like you, baby. Not at all."

"I know."

"And there's nothing I can do?"

He placed his hand on hers. This wasn't the time to alienate her. They were back together, and he had no intention of doing or saying anything that might jeopardize her homecoming. "You've already done it, baby. You came back to me."

Despite his joy, he could never forget the last few days. The trip to the Parkway Towers. The .45 gripped in his hand. And, of course, the dog. Especially the dog. And what the animal had done.

How she had comforted him, taken his mind off his nightmare. How she had saved his life.

Lastly, how quickly and easily the dog had buried herself so deeply inside his heart. So much so, in fact, that while on the way to the hospital, he could think only of Morgan meeting the dog when they returned home and making her an integral part of their family.

But now that they had returned and found her gone, he realized that this happiness was just not meant to be. And that life once again had taken a turn he had not been prepared to face.

"Maybe she's in the kitchen..." Morgan sounded hopeful.

Despite his doubts, he moved quickly down the hall and stopped in the kitchen doorway, his gaze settling on the empty room. He found that he could not stop gawking at the water dish, which was still more than half full. Next to it, the dry food he had dumped in her bowl before leaving for the hospital hadn't been touched. The sight of it made him incredibly sad.

Bella was gone. And after listening to Morgan's explanation of her hallucination, he wasn't even certain the dog was ever here in the first place.

But she *was*, wasn't she? She walked right up to him on Broadway Avenue just before he was about to commit murder. She jumped into his car, rode with him to this apartment, slept in his bed, drank from the water dish, even ate some of his black forest ham. She talked to him in her own special way, smiled at him, swished her nub at him, and sent him images that had saved his heart and soul and, ultimately, his life.

Yes. She was here. But now she was gone, and a large chunk of his heart throbbed as if he'd been slammed in the chest with a sledgehammer.

"Are you okay, baby?" Morgan moved closer.

Owen could not reply. There were no words he could find that would sufficiently express his feelings, his grief. The love of his life had finally come back to him, but the beautiful animal that had helped him survive had vanished. There were no visible signs whatsoever that a dog had even been here with him.

"I'm wondering what actually happened to you while I was gone," Morgan said.

"I'm wondering the same thing. But I'm telling you right now that a sweet, beautiful dog came to me three nights ago and kept me company at a time when I really needed some brightness in my life. I don't know what would have happened if she hadn't shown up."

"The woman in my dream must have sent her. I truly believe that."

He couldn't think of anything else that would explain what had happened. Even so, too many questions remained unanswered. "But where did she come from? I mean, where were the two of them? You don't know, do you?"

"I think they might have been together before we met one another. But as far as where they were, I have no idea. Who knows what really happened?"

"She was here, baby. I talked to her, touched her. She touched me, too. Smiled at me. Listened to

208

me. Swished her furry little tail at me. Even talked to me in her own mysterious way." He simply could not accept the fact that the dog had been a hallucination.

"I'm sure she was here, Owen."

He wondered if she was humoring him. "Really?"

Morgan nodded and pressed harder against him.

Owen turned back to the water dish and food bowl. He could feel tears gathering. "She was very special. Hallucination or not, she was beautiful."

Morgan grasped his hand tightly. He took it, and the warmth emanating from her warmed him, making him feel less anxious. But the fact remained. The wonderful dog that had somehow provided him the much needed sunlight that had made the darkness of his life disappear was no longer with him, and he felt just as lonely and as sad as he had when Morgan had been taken from him.

Things that hadn't made sense until now had grown clearer. The dog's perception of things. Her expressions, reactions to him and the situation. His nagging feeling that Bella clearly understood exactly what was going on. That special warmth he felt when her paw touched his hand. And, of course, the real reason the vet's chip scanner hadn't worked right.

"The woman in your dream...what did she tell you about Bella?"

"I'm sorry, but I just can't remember very much. However, I kinda think my friend actually knew Bella would help you."

He could feel more tears filling his eyes but made no effort to wipe them away. "She stopped me from killing Hargrove. Aside from giving me much needed company and companionship, she somehow made life worth living once again. Just last night, she gave me a warning that quite possibly saved my life."

"What sort of warning?"

"She insisted I walk away from Hargrove's apartment and get back in the elevator."

Morgan frowned.

"Something wrong?"

"I can't really tell for sure, but it seems like there's definitely something trying to work its way free in my mind. All I do know is that I sensed something dark and cold the moment you mentioned that man's apartment."

"Some memory trying to wriggle free?"

"Just something very vague. But it seems important."

"Maybe it'll come back later, when you're no longer obsessing over it."

"Maybe..."

He turned back to the empty kitchen and sighed brokenly. "She changed me, baby."

"I know."

"Does it show?"

"I'll put it this way. I'm really surprised you didn't kill that man. Not that long ago, you would have."

"I really think Bella did something to me. Something good."

210

"It sounds like she awakened things in you that needed to be awakened. And got rid of things that didn't need to be there in the first place."

Owen sighed. "Well, she's gone now. And I didn't even get the chance to thank her."

She gently touched his cheek. "I kinda think that wherever she is now, she knows how you feel."

EPILOGUE

The next day, Owen drove Morgan to the public park at Lake Nona, where they first met eight years earlier at the company picnic.

It was a warm, sunny, cloudless day. When they first arrived, they were both pleased that they had the park mostly to themselves. Aside from an occasional jogger using the dirt path encircling the woods and a younger couple and two small children having a picnic down near the lake, the large area was deserted.

Owen helped Morgan out of the Challenger. She was experiencing lingering pain in her back and right hip and needed his assistance. Once she had regained her balance, they went down the grassy slope that led to the lake, where dozens of Ospreys perched silently in trees, waiting patiently for the prospects of a hearty lunch from activity in the water. Holding Morgan carefully by the arm, Owen led her leisurely along the path that followed the contours of the lake, which led to a grove filled with vacant picnic tables, a couple of privies, and several weathered pavilions.

"This is nice," Morgan said as she shuffled along, holding on to his arm. "It doesn't seem like we've been together eight years, does it?"

He thought of the last three months and discovered that even though Morgan had only been back with him the last few days, it felt like an eternity had passed since the morning the hospital called to tell him she had come out of her coma. "Sometimes it does."

She squeezed his arm. "It happened, baby. It was horrible, but it happened, and now it's over. We need to get over it, don't we?"

He nodded, but he knew he would never forget the morning she had come out of her coma. Bella entered his thoughts once again, and that same heavy sadness that had slammed through him before slammed through him once again. The blow wasn't quite as bad this time, but it hurt just as much. His longing for her grew once again, and he realized for the umpteenth time just how much he deeply missed her.

"That was a real shame what happened to that young woman," Morgan said.

For a moment he wondered what she was talking about. When it registered, he recalled the shock he had felt when the two of them saw it on Fox News the night before. Karma had dealt Hargrove a devastating blow. The newscast had said Hargrove, the only suspect, had been apprehended in the apartment and was arrested at the scene.

The image of Bella urging him to get back in the elevator returned, making him realize yet again just how fortunate he was. According to the news story, Hargrove had shot the woman just minutes after Owen and Bella had left the building. *She really did save my life*, he thought, and he felt himself softening once again when he realized he would never see her again.

"I guess we'll never know what actually happened." Morgan sounded pensive. "The news

213

report said the two of them worked at the same company, so I guess there's a good chance it might have been a romance thing gone bad."

"You sound skeptical."

She smiled. "The only thing I care about is that Bella got you out of there in time."

"If it hadn't been for her, I would have most likely been shot."

Around the bend, Owen glimpsed the magnificent sight and gasped. Then stopped dead in his tracks.

Bella was sitting in the middle of the dirt path, watching him. The late morning sun cast a special light on her, giving her golden-brown coat a shimmering glow, and her big brown eyes sparkled. As always, she seemed to be smiling at him.

"Baby?" Morgan was watching him closely. "You okay?"

Tears gathered in his eyes as he gawked at the beautiful vision. He knew he was facing a hallucination. Bella had come back to see him one last time.

I'll never forget you, he thought as he gazed at the beautiful sight. *And I'll never be able to thank you enough.*

The animal smiled and said, "*Woof!*" in reply. In the next instant, a sparkling light behind her flickered, blending in with the shimmering glow cast down upon her.

In the next moment, she was gone.

"Baby?" Morgan looked worried.

He glanced up at the cloudless blue sky but saw no sign of her.

214

"What happened?"

He couldn't reply. All he could do was gaze longingly at the empty path, where the hallucination of the beautiful animal had been only moments ago.

"Was it her?" she whispered cautiously. "Was it…Bella?"

He nodded, and a tear drifted down his cheek.

She stared nervously at him.

"I'm okay," he replied, gently squeezing her hand.

"You're sure?"

"I'm sure." He kissed her lightly on the lips. "Let's go home now."

"She came back to say goodbye."

"Yes. She did."

"I was hoping she would."

"Really?"

"It helped, didn't it?"

"Very much so."

Morgan smiled and stroked his arm.

He smiled back. "Tell me something."

"Yes?"

"What do we do with all that dog food I bought?"

She shrugged. "I guess we could either donate it or use it wisely."

"Wisely?"

"Maybe we should consider adopting a dog…"

"Are you serious?"

She nodded and kissed him.

"It's not too soon? After Hannah?"

"I think that after Bella, the time will be just perfect."

"I was hoping you'd say something like that."
Still smiling and clinging tightly to one another, they turned and walked back up the slope.

And God said, "I will send them without wings
so no one suspects they are angels."
--Unknown

216

OTHER WORKS BY DAVID BERARDELLI

THE APPRENTICE
THE WAGON DRIVER
STEPPING OUT OF MY GRAVE
ESCAPE CLAUSE
FATAL INNOCENCE
COLORS
IN ANOTHER REALM
BEYOND RECOGNITION
THE NIGHTMARE COLLECTOR
HIDDEN
BEYOND GUILT
A RIPPLE IN TIME
YESTERDAY'S JOURNEY
ENLIGHTENMENT
REDEMPTION

Titles available through:
Fiction4All
www.fiction4all.com

217